Sparking ARES

ROYAL BASTARDS MC

USA TODAY BESTELLING AUTHOR

KRISTINE ALLEN

Published in the United States of America. First published January 3, 2023.
Cover Design: Glenna Maynard, Gchelle Designs
Photographer: Wander Aguiar
Cover Model: Thane; image licensed for use by Wander Aguiar Photography
Editing: Darlene Tallman

Paperback ISBN-13: 978-1-953318-10-7

ROYAL BASTARDS MC SERIES

Featured Characters:

Dragon, Wrecker, and Animal from Liberty Parker's
Cedar Creek, TX Chapter

To Kristin… for being an awesome friend and keeping me from going under more times than you know.

Sparking
ARES
ROYAL BASTARDS MC

PROLOGUE

Age eighteen

"I'll see you tomorrow night," Renee said before she kissed me, then climbed off the back of my bike. As she walked up to her front door, she shot a coy smirk over her shoulder. I couldn't have kept the grin off my face if I tried.

"I'll pick you up at eight," I called after her. She gave me a wave and went inside.

My old '78 XLH-1000 Sportster rumbled through the dark streets as I headed home. The muggy Minnesota night had ended with a hot and heavy make out session with Renee and her agreeing to go out with me. Not that I ever had trouble getting laid, they usually only wanted me for that. So, yeah, it made me feel good that a white-trash guy like myself had bagged the prettiest cheerleader on the squad. She'd be leaving in the fall, but it would be fun while it lasted.

Fuck all those pricks I graduated with that looked down their nose at me. No, I wasn't loaded like they were, and I wouldn't be going to some Ivy League college, but I didn't care. My uncle Dice hooked me up with a job at his bike repair shop and I was in love. Dice wasn't my blood uncle, but he was good friends with my mom's oldest brother and had been like family for as long as I could remember. The smell of grease and oil with the weight of a wrench in my hand was all I needed. Tearing down a motor and putting it back together was enough to give me a goddamn woody.

Okay, maybe that was a stretch, but I really did fucking love it.

The Sportster had been rotting in an old lady's barn when Dice found it and brought it back to the shop. He and I had rebuilt the 75th anniversary edition bike and he'd given it to me for my eighteenth birthday. It wasn't the biggest or baddest bike out there, but it kept girls like Renee wanting a chance to fuck me and be seen on the back. Okay, my looks didn't hurt either. Between the two, I shamelessly used them to my advantage.

My mom always said I looked like my dad's mini me. When I was little, I thought it was cool. When I got older, I hated it. Over the years, my face was a constant reminder to my mom of the man she loved and lost. It also pissed my stepdad off because I was a little kick in the balls when he looked at me—the living reminder that my mom would never love him as much as me or my father.

But when I discovered girls, I realized my looks had been a blessing in disguise.

Joel, my stepdad, was a narcissistic asshole. Two things he couldn't stand—the fact that he wasn't the most important person in her life, and that I looked like the man that still held her heart from the grave.

Initially, his petty jealousy was tolerable—until he lost his job and started drinking heavily. Then he started being verbally and mentally abusive to my mom. They argued all the time.

Eventually, it turned physical—of course only when I wasn't around. The first time I went after him I was about thirteen. He whooped my ass, and my mom begged me to never do that again. Then I got older and bigger. Each time I caught my mom putting makeup on her bruised cheek, I told her I was going to give him a taste of his own medicine.

She adamantly refused, and told me she was afraid he would kill me. I wanted to say not before I killed him first, but I kept my mouth shut. If I ever caught him in the act, there would be no stopping me.

When I rolled up and cut my engine, I could hear them screaming through the thin walls of the trailer. The one we moved into after Joel couldn't get another job because he was always drunk. At the time, I was young and didn't care that we had to move. We were in the back of the trailer park that butted up to the woods. I spent countless hours exploring and simply enjoying the sun dappled area. Something about the quiet calmness called to me—stilled the chaos in my head and eventually our home.

"Jesus," I muttered, glancing next door at the open windows. I knew damn well the neighbors wouldn't call the cops because half of them were cooking meth, but still. I was so tired of the fighting.

Except, when I opened the door, that was the last straw. The door slamming behind me didn't so much as registered in Joel's pickled brain. Nor did he notice me vault over the back of the couch because I wasn't going around.

"Who the fuck was he?" I heard him yell as he landed a punch.

"Joel, I told you he works with me!" my mom cried as she tried to protect her already battered face from his heavy fists.

A roar erupted from deep in my soul as I threw him back. He landed on the floor, and I closed in on him. "You wanna hit someone, Joel? You hit me! Come on," I taunted.

"You little fucking punk," he rasped and launched back to his feet. In my anger, I missed the switchblade until it was too late. Thankfully, my reflexes kicked in and I was able to bring an arm up to block him. It didn't stop him from slicing my shoulder open instead.

"Joel! Stop!" Mom shrieked as she jumped on his back and wrapped her arms around his neck. Her tiny frame was no match for him, and he ripped her off and threw her to the ground. She moaned, and he advanced on her, blade dripping with my blood.

Something inside me ripped apart and I saw red—literally.

Then I blacked out, my actions no longer my own. Yet they were.

"Memphis! You need to go to the woods. Hide until I come for you," my mom whispered with panic flashing in her pretty blue eyes. Blood was smeared on her face, and I had no idea if it was hers, mine, or his.

Feeling disoriented, I blinked as my chest heaved and I looked around at the blood that splattered across the TV and the walls. The crumpled form on the living room floor was near unrecognizable. Except the vicious slashes that shredded his flesh brought flashbacks of power, claws, and sharp teeth.

Confused, I glanced at my mother. "What did I do?"

With a shaking hand, she reached for me. The feel of her stroking my head brought a rumbling purr from deep within my chest. She stood and, using the walls, stumbled through the kitchen and down the short hall to the laundry room. I heard the back door open, and I followed.

"Memphis, you need to go! Get out of here!" she insisted, and I was hurt at her seemingly angry words.

It wasn't until I jumped down the stairs landing on all fours that I realized—I landed on *all fours*. Blood covered the golden fur where I should've had hands. I jumped sideways and caught a glimpse of a long dark-tipped tail that I spun trying to see.

"Go!" my mom angrily repeated and threw a shoe out the door at me. Unable to process, I took off at a lope into the dark trees. I didn't go far, because I was scared and worried. Using the blood-soaked claws on my *four* feet, I climbed a tree that gave me a view of the trailer but hid me in the branches.

Lean muscles trembled as I laid on the thick branch and

rested my head on my paws. My mind was spinning, and nothing made sense, but fuck if I wasn't a giant cat.

It wasn't long before I heard the rumble of a motorcycle. From my perch, I saw the back patch that I immediately recognized.

The Royal Bastards.

It was my actual uncle Frank, and I was tempted to go to him, but I had no clue what was going on and hello… I had turned into a fucking mountain lion.

He wasn't inside for long when he came out the back door, Mom on his heels.

"Leslie, I told you he needed to be around his family. Just because Kyle was human, it didn't mean Memphis would be. Our family has always been shifters and you damn well knew it was a possibility."

"He hadn't shown any signs, Frank. None! I'd been watching. But I wasn't stupid, I was only taking it one day at a time. Look what happened to the rest of our family. You can't blame me for wishing he would be like Kyle and not us."

"Jesus, Les, you know it can be different for everyone. You should've given the kid a head's up—that's why I wanted him to come live with me. Sometimes it doesn't manifest until the person goes through a significantly stressful time. That stupid piece of shit you married was bound to push him. Now we need to find him before he totally freaks and does something stupid."

Too late for that, I was already freaking the hell out.

"Joel wasn't always like that," Mom argued, but it sounded

weak. Maybe Joel wasn't abusive at the beginning, but he was always a selfish dick.

My uncle Frank stopped below the tree I was perched in, then looked right up at me. "Boy? You can come down. I'm here to help, but I need to talk to you."

I blinked and stared, but he patiently waited. Finally, I descended—my claws digging into the coarse bark of the tree. With a soft thud as my weight hit the ground, I dropped the final few feet. Warily, I watched him. My tail flicked nervously as I waited, slightly crouched.

"Memphis, I need you to listen to me. You can change back, but I want you to relax and focus. It's a matter of telling your body what you want it to do." He was calm and patient with me as he talked me through everything.

I should've gone to prison for killing my stepfather.

The reason I didn't is complicated. It all boils down to who you know—and my mom evidently knew some pretty powerful people. A bunch of guys showed up that night with a van. They introduced themselves as my uncle Frank's brothers from the chapter down in Ankeny, Iowa. They parked by the back door and in a crazy amount of time, they had erased every sign of Joel's demise.

They spoke quietly with my uncle Frank, and I knew they were talking about me, because they kept glancing my way.

When all was said and done, Mom and I went to live with Uncle Frank. He taught me how to control myself so I wouldn't change unexpectedly. He explained the necessary precautions I needed to take. When I inevitably wanted to join his club a couple of years later, he shook his head.

"Son, I don't want this life for you, but I'm not gonna tell you how to live. If you're dead set on it, I'd prefer you joined Dice's club. They're just down across the border and they live a little uh... tamer... than we do." Frank stroked his beard as he spoke.

"But I want to be with you and the brothers here," I countered. They'd all become like family over the past couple of years.

"I get it, but I think you need to be with Dice and the Demented Sons. Live a normal life, ride your bike, and leave that shit in the trailer behind you once and for all," he explained.

I ended up doing as he said, and Dice was happy to have me as a "nephew" and then a brother in the club.

Except what happened that night was something that I'd never forget, and I'd never forgive myself for.

I was a monster.

ONE

Ares

"DANCING IN THE SKY"—DANI AND LIZZY

It was my job to sit in the van down the road and watch the cameras. We had hacked into them with the help of Facet, one of our brothers from the Ankeny, IA chapter. I wasn't a tech guy, but I could handle that. What I hadn't planned on, was everything going to shit at once.

Raptor was inside confronting his ex when a sleek Bugatti Chiron roared up the driveway and skidded to a stop. Tigger was watching the front door and one guy shouldn't have been a problem for him. Except neither of us realized the guy had a taser in his hand. He had Tigger face down on the ground and he was inside before either of us saw it coming.

I tried to notify everyone, but my comms glitched.

"Fuck!" I shouted as I threw the headset to the floor of the van and clambered out. As I ran, I chambered a round. Blade and Torque must've heard the car pull up because they had tactically moved to the front of the house. Gator came from the other side. Problem was, they didn't know what had happened. They saw me running and I pointed toward where Tigger lay crumpled by the steps. They reached him before I did, so I didn't pause.

"What the fuck, kid?" Gator grumbled as he checked Tigger.

"My goddamn comms didn't work!" I ground out as I sped past them and through the front door. Since they were with Tigger, I didn't bother stopping.

Blade followed me toward the main entrance.

As I ran down the hall, I could see into the room where Raptor stood with his hands out. When the gunshot rang out, it was like a lightning bolt hit me. Every fiber of my being exploded and ripped apart—along with my clothes as I shifted into the mountain lion that lurked within.

It was a strange sensation to become an entirely different creature.

Caged too long, the big cat was not only in instant protective mode, but it was out for blood. Raptor was my president, but he was more. He took me in, knowing I had demons that haunted me. He gave me my probationary patch when others would've made me prospect regardless of the leeway they were granted to open a new chapter.

He promised me retribution.

I'd kill for him—and I did.

Snarling mixed with the man's screams until there was nothing recognizable of the piece of shit who had tried to shoot Raptor. Like a flashback, blood was everywhere. I trembled from the adrenaline. Torn between a sick horror at the savagery I'd unleashed, and riding on the rush of power, I backed away from the mangled body.

Though I thought I was, I hadn't been prepared. Because killing someone wasn't what I had a hard time with, it was how I did it.

After I'd shredded the asshole that was married to my prez's ex, I freaked out a little and ran. I hadn't intended on letting the beast within escape again. Twice I'd killed someone in my rage. The first time because my mother was being threatened—this time, my president. Jesus, I'd heard that shot fired and lost it. Shame filled me at my lack of control.

Corded and sleek muscles, long denied, drove me forward as my legs ate up the miles. The compound was where I instinctually went after the incident. Deep in the thick cedar and live oaks to the back of the property that we hadn't cleared. My razor-sharp claws gouged into the bark as I practically flew up the tree. Up on one of the highest branches that would hold my weight, I'd crouched in uncertainty. Waiting for what? I had no idea.

"I know you're out here, kid," I heard One Short call out as he sat on a cedar stump and lit a cigarette. He took a deep drag before slowly letting it out over his head.

The leaves on the limb rustled as I shifted my weight, and he looked up.

"You're not in trouble, if that's what you're worried about. Raptor called me and asked me to check to see if you were here somewhere. I replayed the cameras and saw you go through where you discovered the opening in the fence. Come on down. It's okay," he practically crooned, trying his damnedest to get me to leave my perch.

Swallowing hard, I carefully made my way down the tree until I could leap to the ground. Watching him cautiously, I sat on my haunches trembling in anticipation, ready to run if need be.

"Damn," he whispered as he stood and dropped a backpack on the ground. "You're really somethin,' aren't you?"

Unmoving, I blinked at him and then my tail flicked back and forth in agitation.

"Those eyes... holy shit... gotta say, you're one badass kitty-cat." I hissed and snarled at being called a fucking kitty-cat.

"Whoa! Easy, now," he warily called out as he held his hands out in front of him—as if that would stop me if I wanted to go after his ass. Slowly, he brought out his phone. "I'm just calling Raptor to let him know you're safe."

I waited while he quietly made the call.

It wasn't overly long before the big hawk swooped down and landed with a soft thud.

Eyes wide, I watched as he seemed to melt and morph. It seemed like I blinked, and he was a man. I wondered if I looked like that when I changed. Calmly, he unrolled some clothing he had brought in his talons and dressed.

"Ares, if you're able to change back, One Short has some of your clothes in the bag." He lifted his chin and motioned over his shoulder. One Short was gingerly holding up the pack.

Now that I'd calmed down, I felt more able to make the transition back to myself. It was a painful process that left me kneeling on the ground, hands braced in front of me, and teeth clenched as I moaned. Once I caught my breath, I held out a hand for the backpack. Keeping my gaze on the ground, I quickly pulled on my clothes.

Though my uncle had explained the shifting process and I had shown him I was able to make the transition back and forth, I didn't do it again. Over the years, I had tried to keep myself from losing my cool, because I didn't have as much control when I was full of rage. Until the day Tasha was killed. Thankfully, I'd made it out into the woods that day before I couldn't control it anymore. I never would've been able to explain that to my brothers in the DSMC.

Once I was clothed, I looked up into my president's eyes, expecting disappointment or anger. Instead, I saw compassion and understanding. Shaken, I stepped back.

"Memphis, I swear you're not on my shit list. I'm actually grateful. You saved my life. Because I have no doubt after he shot Falina, he would've fired again. There was no way I would've been able to pull my weapon in time. Especially with her falling into me. For that, I thank you."

His calling me by my given name cracked my shell just a bit. I didn't like that because it made me feel weak.

"Let's go back to the clubhouse. We need to check on Tigger and regroup."

Unable to speak for fear that I would break down, I nodded.

Several days later, I was called into the chapel. I arrived early and sat there lost in my thoughts.

Where my mind often went... regrets.

When I'd met Tasha, I was immediately hooked, but I knew she deserved better than me. Which was why I kept her at an arm's distance, though it killed me. That didn't mean I didn't watch over her and know her every move when she was in the same room. When she'd began dancing at the The Emerald Shamrock, I'd nearly lost my fucking mind.

I'd gotten my ass in a sling more times than I cared to admit because of men touching her or her doing a lap dance for extra money. If I would've been a better man, I would've claimed her and taken care of her, so she didn't need to dance. Instead, I'd stolen little moments with her that left me even more frustrated.

The day she died in my arms, I wanted to die myself. Then rage took over and I had a burning vengeance that simmered inside me—waiting to be let loose on the person or people responsible.

Snow was the only one who knew my secret and he'd given me permission to talk to Venom and Raptor. I tried to hire them to find whoever had killed Tash so I could get my pound of flesh. They told me that wasn't how they did things.

After that, I made a decision. I'd ended up leaving the

DSMC and joining the RBMC in Dallas so I could do the job myself. Soap had ceased to exist and over my six months of probation, Ares had come to be. The need for blood and payback raced in my veins.

I'd been biding my time and proving myself as Facet dug into the shooting.

The unremarkable folder hit the table with a slap, and I jumped as I was abruptly pulled from my musings. I stared at it a moment before lifting my gaze to Raptor. My heart took off at a gallop that I tried to rein in—in case I was wrong, and this wasn't the info I'd been waiting over a year and a half for.

"What's this?" I cautiously asked. Uncertain, I didn't know if I wanted to open it.

"You wanted your revenge," Raptor rumbled, but the angry blaze in his eyes gave me pause. I couldn't think of a fucking thing I'd done wrong. I'd completed every task I'd been assigned over the past six months of my probationary period. Not once had I balked or hesitated. Yet Raptor was furious and fighting to contain it.

When I slowly reached for the folder, his massive hand splayed over it. "You make it hurt—because I want my revenge too."

Confused, I silently nodded. He removed his hand, and I drew the manilla folder closer. Inside, the first page had the image of a guy that looked familiar. Before I could ask who it was, I flipped to the next page.

George Horacio.

It listed his multiple known addresses, which included the blueprints to what was noted as his principal residence—a massive home in Highland Park. Going over the rest of the details, I read that he owned a plethora of businesses around the country. Everything from restaurants to strip clubs and even a few sex clubs.

That's how I knew him.

When I was with the DSMC, he bought out our competitor and stole a few of the girls that danced at our strip club, The Emerald Shamrock. He was a dick, and we knew he was up to something but he was smart and we could never pin anything on him.

"This is who killed Tasha." It wasn't a question. His statement suddenly clicked—this was my revenge. My blood began to boil, but I kept my shit in check. "But what do you mean, you want your revenge too?"

"Because this is also the guy that was fucking with Sage and my old chapter. He takes over strip clubs, gets the dancers hooked on drugs, and turns them into prostitutes. The Ankeny chapter found out he was the one who ran Sage off the road up there and that he planned to make her his personal plaything."

Jesus.

"Okay. I won't let you down, Prez. I promise you."

"I know you won't." The stern stare he gave me told me if I fucked this up, *I* was fucked. "You memorize that info because it doesn't leave this room and Phoenix will be incinerating it when you're done. Before you execute anything, I want you to brief the chapter on the plan."

"Got it." Personally, I would've liked to go in and put a bullet between his eyes. But Raptor wanted him to suffer.

For hours, I sat in the chapel pouring over the information. I studied the blueprints, his businesses, his family. By the end of it, I knew his dad left them for his twenty-one-year-old secretary when George was fourteen. His mom remarried Simon Cole, billionaire widower with a young daughter, a year later. The daughter was now twenty-three. She was also staying with George, and he seemed to keep close tabs on her.

I had my plan.

Tasha, I'm going to avenge you.

TWO

Ember

"PERFECT INSANITY"—DISTURBED

It was the day after Christmas and Dad and Rhonda were leaving this morning for their New Year's cruise to celebrate their twentieth anniversary. They would fly to Europe to take a Mediterranean cruise, then tour Italy and France.

"Yes, that one," I told Rhonda as she held up a red dress in one hand and a black dress in the other.

"The red?" she asked, peeking around it.

"Absolutely. It will look phenomenal with your hair." Rhonda had sleek dark hair with a single, thick streak of gray that came off her widow's peak. I knew she'd had some plastic surgery over the years, but I didn't hold it against her. She rocked the hell out of it, and she was good to my dad. Plus, she had been the best stepmom a girl could ask for.

"I've been wondering if I should color this," she mused as she fingered the silver chunk.

"God, no! It's sexy as hell."

She giggled and shook her head at me. We both turned to the patio doors that Dad entered. He'd been making last minute calls for work—go figure. The man wasn't necessarily a workaholic, but he was definitely hands-on with the oil fields he and my uncle owned.

Henry Mason wasn't actually my uncle—he was my dad's cousin. My dad's father and Henry's mom were siblings. They both had been only children. Except where I had been my dad's only child, born later in his life, Henry had five girls and one boy.

My parents had been trying for years and the doctors had advised them not to continue since they were older, but they wanted a baby. To know I'd killed my mother had weighed heavy on me, though my dad swore I was her last gift to him.

"Rhonda, we have thirty minutes before we need to be out of here," Dad announced while tapping on his Rolex. He already had his bags by the door. They'd been packed since last night.

"I'm just making a few last-minute clothing swaps, Honey," she replied before she stood on her tip-toes to kiss his cheek, then ruffled his steel-gray hair. My dad's smile brought out the crinkles by his eyes and made him look years younger. Both of them were good-looking and they made a striking couple.

Though my mom had died when I was born, I knew my dad had loved her like crazy. It was part of the reason he never had me call Rhonda, "Mom." I still thought of her as my mom, though. It also didn't mean that he wasn't crazy about Rhonda. One day, I hoped to have a relationship like they had.

"Is Giselle coming to spend New Year's with you?" Rhonda asked as she zipped her suitcase.

"No. She ended up going to Paris with Blaine." Blaine was Giselle's brother that was the second youngest. The rest of the siblings were all older and long-since married.

Which meant I was on my own or I was stuck here with George. Our parents had gotten married when I was three. Not that I really remembered much of it since I was so little, but I sure remembered George. I'd had a crush on him for as long as I could remember. At least until I was old enough to realize he was essentially my brother, and it would be weird to marry him like I'd always imagined.

"Why don't you go out with some of your girl friends?" Rhonda asked, worry in her soft green eyes. I could tell that she was having second thoughts about leaving.

"Maybe," I replied with a bright grin.

"Well, at least George will be around," my dad said, giving me a kind smile.

"I guess," I grumbled. That was always an option. He had invited me over for the weekend, but I hadn't decided.

He was always protective of me growing up. Except it had gotten worse when I went to high school. College—astronomically terrible. He had hired a bodyguard for me and any time I tried to see someone, he sabotaged it. The rationale he always gave me was that he didn't want a guy taking advantage of me because of who we were. If Dallas, Texas had royalty, it was my dad's family. George's family were mere millionaires to my father's billions. Insert eye roll.

Seriously, the money had never been anything but a curse as far as I was concerned. Giselle and Blaine were my only real friends. Mostly because we all knew that we could trust each other, and we weren't trying to be friends for the money.

My dad had been touched by George's protective streak, but I don't think he realized the extent of it. I had little to no life back then. And I hated his friends. They always looked at me like I was their next meal.

Until I learned how to sneak out of the apartment my dad paid for while I attended UT. I'd gotten so good at subterfuge and changing my appearance, I probably could've gotten a job as a CIA operative. Okay, maybe that's a bit of an exaggeration, but I finally had a life. Well, I did until I graduated and then Dad brought me home to live.

Twenty-three and living with my dad wasn't where I wanted to be.

"Well, if you decide to go to George's, Lowell will be around until New Year's Eve, and you can have him drive you over." Dad reminded me.

Lowell had been with us since my mom was still alive. He was like a surrogate uncle, but I knew he'd be spending the holiday with his family, and I wasn't inviting myself there. Nor did I really feel like being alone over the holiday.

George's it was.

God, I hoped none of his creepy-ass friends were there.

George had been more than happy to have me there for the holiday—he just didn't know I smuggled my cat with me. I'd gone upstairs and unpacked my bag in the room he kept for me for when I stayed with him. I paused by the window to gaze out at George's gorgeous pool, wishing it wasn't cold and rainy. The overcast sky was dark and dreary. I sighed, then decided to forgo the nap I'd told George I was going to take.

"Be good," I quietly told my cat, Mushu as I stroked his silky head. I'd already made sure he knew where his food, water, and the disposable litter box were. He stared at me with his judging blue eyes set in his dark-seal mask and a faint purr hummed for a moment. His tiny little blessing for me—his peasant. Closing the door to keep Mr. Mu where he was safe from George's disdain, I giggled and went downstairs to look for my brother.

His voice carried down the hall from his office, but I couldn't make out what he was saying to determine if it was a business call. He owned a plethora of restaurants and night clubs all over the country and seemed to always be on the go. If he was dealing with that, I didn't want to bother him. In my Vans, I quietly padded down the hall and paused by the cracked door.

"I have a special treat for you when you get here. It should make up for the loss you suffered on our investment in Iowa."

"And how do you know I'll be interested in anything you have for me? Unless it's my money." The man's accented voice carried into the hall from the call he had on speakerphone.

"Oh, I think you'll find her to your liking. Tiny, blonde, lean, big tits but young-looking. Ring a bell?" My face flamed at George's description that I knew right away was me.

"Really… are we talking about who I think we're talking about?" The man suddenly seemed riveted whereas before he'd seemed bored.

"Yes."

"You adamantly denied me before. What changed?"

George sighed. "I'm aware I refused you before, but I'm trying to make this right. You know I don't have the ability to refund your investment at this moment in time. Stop by when you get into town tomorrow and I'll have her waiting for you. You just have to get her out of the country—until you have her married and under control. Unless you don't want her trust fund. If that's the case, she can't ever see the light of day."

What the hell was he talking about? I thought he had more money than God. At least that was the impression he gave.

Wait.

Trust fund?

Things started to click and the "her" he described as one would a car they were selling, sounding sickeningly like me. But that couldn't be right. George and his friends were a little creepy, but that was way worse.

"Well, well, well. I guess I'll swing by." The man practically oozed his satisfaction with the offer.

"Perfect. See you soon."

I heard my brother's irritated sigh before I pushed into

the room, blazing mad. He better hope I was jumping to conclusions. "What the hell was that all about?"

Initially, he stood and appeared placating as he rounded the desk. "You shouldn't listen in on people's private conversations. You obviously misconstrued what you heard."

"Misconstrued?" I parroted in disbelief. My entire image of him had shattered. "You described me to someone on the phone like I was being offered up as a consolation prize, you sick fuck! I heard you tell him he had to take me out of the country and marry me! Fuck. You. I'm leaving. I never should've come here. After all these years and I find out I don't even *know* you."

Tears welled in my eyes and my stomach churned as I pulled my phone from the side pocket of my leggings.

I barely got my phone unlocked when I was thrown back and my phone clattered to the tiles. It took some scrambling to remain on my feet. Stunned, it took a moment and the throbbing in my cheek for it to register that he'd hit me.

George. Had. Hit. Me.

"What the fuck? You hit me!" I blurted out, holding a hand to my face. My heart pounded as the word *run* streamed through my head on repeat with each racing beat. Yet, I was in such shock, I was rooted to the spot.

George spun, running his hand through his hair in agitation as he paced. "I'm in a lot of trouble, Ember."

"So, you're using me to soothe someone's ruffled feathers?" I practically shrieked. "I'm not your property and I'm not a *sex doll*. Our parents are *married*! I grew up looking at you like my older brother. I think I'm going to be sick."

"Why do you think I've protected your innocence for so long? Do you think it was because I gave one fuck about you or your precious virtue? You're a commodity, Ember." He sneered and the realization hit that I really didn't know the man I thought of as a brother—at all. Fear began to creep in from the corners of the room to snake up my body and suffocate me.

"What?" I whispered in quiet devastation.

He went back behind his desk and began shuffling through papers and muttering to himself. I thought I caught "dumb bitch" and something about me being his ticket to getting out of "this mess."

"G-G-George?" I stammered as my throat went tight. None of this made sense. I had to be having a bad dream. Something. Anything other than what I thought was going on.

Except before he could answer, the door opened farther, and a man I'd never seen before walked in like he owned the place. Call me an idiot, but if he was the one George had offered me up to, it might not be half bad. Or maybe I'd officially lost my freaking mind.

Cuz holy hell, he was hot. Everything about him screamed "bad boy." My gaze traveled from his piercing blue eyes, over his close-cropped scruff to his pierced nose and ears, to the tattoos on his neck that showed above the plain black hoodie he wore. He was nothing like the few frat boy types I'd been with before. My heart was racing for a completely different reason, and I didn't even know this guy.

At least until I saw the pistols in his hands. One pointed at George and one at me. That had me holding my breath and freezing. Fear that he might catch the slightest movement and impulsively put a bullet in me kept me stone-still.

This was officially a nightmare. This couldn't be real. I'd actually gone to sleep upstairs, and I was dreaming all of this in some technicolor head trip. My brother had an insanely tight security system.

George made a nearly imperceptible move toward the edge of his desk.

"Don't," the man warned as he moved like a wraith and raised the pistol until it was pressed to my temple.

George put his hands up immediately and at first, I thought I'd been wrong, and he was trying to protect me.

"What the fuck do you want?" George snapped and my eyes popped wide.

The man darkly chuckled.

"Well, you see, I came here to kill her." He motioned to me with his chin before he calmly finished his cold reply. "It was convenient that she was in the same room. I didn't even have to go looking to drag her in front of you. I wanted you know what it's like to watch someone you love die in your arms. Then I was going to kill you."

That explained why he wasn't hiding what he looked like. I sucked in a sharp breath but tried not to make any sudden moves. The entire situation was ridiculous. First, George offered me to his friend for my trust fund and to be God only knew what, then a handsome stranger barged in and announced he was going to kill me. Tears of frustration and helplessness broke past the dam and trickled down my cheeks.

"Except I think it might hurt you more to know that I'm

taking your little sister from you. I think instead of killing her in front of you, I'm going to take her. Then I'm going to fuck her in ways she's never dreamed of—until she's crying and screaming. With each thrust of my cock, she'll know her pain is all your doing and you'll be here wondering if she's still alive. With each breath you take, you'll be looking over your shoulder wondering when I'm coming back for you." The words were spoken in a deadly cold tone and my heart clenched in terror as each one sunk in.

Things had gone from bad to worse.

THREE

Ares

"PERFECT INSANITY"—DISTURBED

J*esus, could this go any more wrong?*

I had a plan. A plan that was going to shit because I was a pussy. What I'd said to George about fucking his sister and hurting her made my stomach churn with nausea. Yet the burning hate kept my mouth shut.

"You're on camera, you know," George finally announced with a smug sneer.

A smirk lifted my lips. "No, I'm not. None of your shit is working." I gave a mock gasp as I popped my eyes wide, and my jaw hung slack.

"You break into my home and tell me you're taking my

sister to torture her. Do you really think you'll get anywhere close to me again?" he ground out between clenched teeth. I'm pretty sure I heard his jaw pop. The man was mad as a motherfucker.

Good.

The corner of my mouth lifted, and I let the demon within shine through before I quietly replied, "Oh, I *know* I can."

"What the fuck do you hope to accomplish?" he snapped. "Pissing me off? Because you have. Or is this about proving you're superior to me in some idiotic way? Or is it money? Is this about a ransom? Because I can pay you."

"It's funny that you think this is about money. Maybe because to you, everything is. But no, it has nothing to do with money. You killed my girl. Putting a bullet between your eyes isn't enough. I could torture you, but that's only physical pain. So instead, I'll take her and use her as I want. It's the pain that keeps on giving." Keeping the muzzle of my gun pressed tight to her head, I placed my extra gun in my side holster, and grabbed her neck as I stepped behind her.

Keeping my insolent gaze locked on his, I leaned my head down to trail my lips over the shell of her ear. Her pulse went wild under my fingers and my cock came to life.

"Hello, Ember," I whispered because after reading Facet's info about her, I knew her name and a fuck-ton of other shit. I'd been watching George's security cameras through the link Facet had set up—waiting patiently for the next time she stayed at his house. "Your pictures don't do you justice. You're so much prettier in person."

A soft, sweet floral scent teased my senses and I had to fight to ignore the feeling of her silky skin against my palm. Suddenly my inner mountain lion stirred.

No, no, no, no, no.

It was then that I knew I was a fucking idiot and Raptor was going to have my ass. Regardless, I couldn't kill her. Tasha's face had flashed in my mind, and I simply couldn't get past that none of my grief or Raptor's anger were this girl's fault. Which was why I made the rash decision to steal her because her brother obviously cared about her. For over a year, I was burning with rage and hate. I believed myself to be heartless and half-dead. Yet, here I was, cracking—failing at my own cold-hearted plan.

"You can't do this." George gritted his teeth and balled his hands. "I've seen you. I will track you down and destroy you."

I barked a humorless laugh. "I can and I will. You call anyone, or follow us and I'll kill her and dump her body out on the road. Oh, and you better watch your back, because I promise you, I'll be coming for you when I'm done with her."

Backing out of the room, I dragged the tiny blonde with me. She was so little, I probably could've tucked her under my arm and carried her. "Don't make a scene," I quietly warned her.

"What the fuck?" Phoenix asked as I came out with her. He and Torque were dressed in head-to-toe black like I was, and waiting out back.

"It's a long story," I muttered as we rushed around the house through the shadows.

"This is bad," Torque muttered.

"Shut up. I fucking know."

By the time we were out by the van I'd driven, I was starting to regret my decision. As a probationary patch, I had been given my patch based on my time with the DSMC and the fact that the Dallas chapter was newly re-opened by Raptor. We were in a building phase which gave him flexibility until he had eight members.

Truthfully, I was only a glorified prospect. Until I was with the club for a year, my patch was easily taken, and I would be busted down to prospect and made to complete a year of prospect time regardless of how long I'd completed of that probationary year. If my fuck up was too bad... I was as good as dead.

"Get in," I demanded. When she paused and didn't move, I picked her up and carefully set her in on the floor, then slammed the door.

The guys piled in the passenger door, and I wasted no time getting the fuck out of there. My jaw was popping as I clenched it. Every so often, I caught their sidelong glances. None of us wanted to talk in front of Ember more than we had.

Several miles down the road, at the dive bar where we'd dropped off their bikes, I let them out. Then I pulled back on the road and it was mere seconds later, they were pulling out of the parking lot as one and speeding up to follow me.

Palms pressed to the expanded metal divider, she practically panted. Then in a voice that was barely above a whisper, she asked, "Do you really plan on doing all that to me?"

Turning a corner, I checked my mirrors. The bikes and I

were the only vehicles moving as we traveled back to the compound on the back highway. I ignored her because I didn't know what the fuck to say.

Finally, I glanced at her in the mirror. If I was as cold as I thought I was, I probably would've done it. At least let her think I would. Except it seemed my heart of ice had defrosted a bit. "No."

She let out a sigh that sounded like relief.

"Do you realize how bad you fucked up?" she asked from where she looked through the expanded metal that separated the front of the van from the back.

"Do I look like I care?" I did because I knew I was in deep shit, but I wasn't telling her that.

"He doesn't give two shits about me," she continued matter-of-factly as if I hadn't spoken. "Not like you think."

"What are you talking about? He never lets you out of his sight. If he's not with you, he has someone watching you—did you know that? That doesn't sound like someone who doesn't care about you."

"Yeah? Well, before you got there tonight, he hit me because I overheard him telling someone they could *have* me. Like I was a jacket or a pair of shoes. Was that you?" she asked, and my surprised gaze met hers in the rearview.

"Me? Did it look like we had any kind of relationship? He doesn't know who I am."

"He will. He's seen you and he has the money to find you," she calmly explained. It was almost eerie. Then she must've sat down. She remained silent the rest of the way and I did the same. My thoughts were jumbled and bouncing around in my head like pinballs.

Once we were through the gates and they were safely closed, I breathed a sigh of relief. Phoenix and Torque parked under the long carport we'd installed along the front of the clubhouse for the bikes. I drove around back and did the same.

Sitting in the quiet van lost in thought, I berated myself. After a minute, I wondered if she was still awake back there. A peek through the divider showed her huddled up, knees to her chest. Reluctantly, I climbed out and went to the back. Prepared for her to jump me or hit me, I slowly opened the door.

Instead, she remained unmoving. Her blonde hair was coming out of the messy bun-thing and hung in her face as she stared forward, ignoring me.

"We're here," I told her.

"Where's here?" she mumbled, still not moving, or looking at me.

"Where we were going," I vaguely replied, trying to bite back the exasperation I was feeling for her and the situation I'd put myself in.

"You gonna tie me up or something?"

"Do I need to?"

"Depends."

"On?"

"On whether I can get out of this place if I run," she truthfully explained as she turned her head to look at me.

"You can't."

"Then, no."

"Well, come on," I told her as I held out a hand. Her wary blue eyes stared at it for what seemed like forever before she uncurled herself and crawled toward me. When she rested her dainty hand in mine, my knees almost buckled at the jolt that hit me. Shaking it off was easier said than done. She climbed down and her gaze darted around the dark compound.

Our breath left steamy little clouds in the air before they dissipated. Too busy looking around to realize I still held her hand, she unknowingly leaned into me for warmth.

A purr rumbled in my chest that I couldn't contain, and my cougar rumbled *mate her*.

Whoa, buddy. Easy there.

As if she'd heard either the purr or the argument I was having in my head with my mountain lion, she stepped back. A short growl of displeasure followed her actions, and she wrapped her arms around herself, appearing frightened.

"A-a-are there w-w-wild animals out here?" she stuttered as she shivered.

"A few, let's go," I grabbed her hand, ignoring that same crackle of awareness, and dragged her along. Her small stature meant she was practically running to keep up with my long-legged stride. I couldn't slow down though, because I'd be tempted to pull her close again.

To her credit, she didn't complain and still kept up. Her gasp had me stopping in my tracks and pulling her into my protective embrace out of instinct. I scanned the area but found nothing amiss.

"What?" I barked.

"The lights!" she squeaked from where her face was buried in my chest thanks to my hand shoving it there.

Confused, I looked around for a spotlight or something to that effect. When I came up with nothing, I glanced down at her. "Where?"

She shoved herself back and pushed the hair that had tumbled free, out of her face. "There!"

That was when it dawned on me that she was talking about the Christmas lights that were still on the cabins in our little camp. Raptor's ol' lady had insisted on them being put up and got Raptor to agree to them being up until after New Year's.

"Jesus, you had me—" I snapped my mouth shut, because I didn't want to admit the tiny pixie had scared the fuck out of me.

"It looks like Santa's Village! Like a bunch of gingerbread houses!" she declared, delight reflecting in her gaze.

Seeing them through her eyes, I could see what she was saying. The corner of my mouth kicked up, but I immediately scowled and propelled her toward my cabin. As I stomped up the stairs, I did it with my hands around the tops of her arms as I lifted her to the top of the small porch.

Reaching around her, I twisted the knob and pushed the door in. Then I grunted, "In."

She cautiously did as I said. I closed the door and leaned against it. Safe in my small domain, I ran my hands down my face in frustration. She stood in the middle of the minuscule home taking it all in.

Looking it over, I realized it wasn't much. The officers

had larger cabins available to them, but the members' cabins were essentially an efficiency apartment. It was enough for me. I had a queen-sized bed in the corner with a single nightstand, a futon, and two barstools that were up to the counter that doubled as a breakfast bar. A TV was mounted to the wall that I could watch from bed or from the futon. A door went to the bathroom that spanned half the width of the end, my closet the other. The bathroom wasn't much, but it had a shower, toilet, and pedestal sink which worked for me.

"Now what?" she asked.

Wasn't that the question of the hour?

I had nothing to say.

"Okaaay. Then, in response to your earlier comment, I think the only reason he had someone watching me was because he planned on benefitting from me."

That got my mouth working.

"Exactly what happened before I got there tonight?"

She explained what she'd overheard, and anger flared to life in my chest.

"So, you think he was protecting his investment?" I incredulously asked.

"Pretty much. Except he obviously doesn't know I ditched my babysitter and snuck out a lot in college." She shrugged and crossed her arms over a chest that was blessedly larger than her frame warranted. "Now, what do you plan on doing with me, pretty boy? Because whether you knew it or not, you actually rescued me."

Well, shit.

The knock on my door was so loud and with such force that I was pretty sure the entire cabin shook.

"And this is where we wrap up the evening and everything completely goes to shit," I muttered as I turned.

The scowling face of my president met mine when I swung the door open. My stomach bottomed out and I swallowed hard. Other than that, I showed no outward sign of my trepidation.

"Outside. Now," he snarled.

Fuck.

I did as I was told, bracing for the impact of his fist.

"What the actual fuck are you doing?" he demanded the second my feet hit the wooden surface.

"Horacio thinks I'm using her to punish him and that I'm going back for him when he least expects it." It sounded lame, even to me, but I wasn't thinking clearly. My actions were spontaneous, impulsive, and reckless and I damn well knew it.

"That wasn't the deal!"

"I understand. I'm going to handle it."

"How?"

"I plan to go back and kill George after he suffers for a while."

"Oh, really."

"Yes."

"No. You bring him here. Now what the fuck are you going to do with *her*? She's basically a prisoner here, and oh, yeah, she can *identify* you. Did you think about that? No. No, you didn't. You said you had what it took. We don't have room in this club for someone who can't get the job done."

My chest ached and panic began to set in. Yeah, I could probably go back to Iowa and the DSMC, but in the Dallas RBMC I was the closest to feeling like I *belonged,* in forever.

"I can get the job done, prez. But Tasha was an innocent victim. She died because we had done the right thing and that piece of shit didn't like it. No matter what kind of shitbag Ember's brother is, she's innocent. And you told me when I joined that we do the dirty work that the law won't—to protect the innocent and to right wrongs. If that's the case, tell me, how do I justify killing her?" My fists curled tighter until my knuckles popped as I tried my damnedest to gain control of myself. The last thing I wanted to do was piss off the president of the club I was holding a probationary patch for—but goddamn I was a mad motherfucker.

Raptor's eyes narrowed and his jaw worked, but he remained silent. Hopefully because he knew I was right.

"Well, I have a better idea," he said through gritted teeth as he pulled his pistol from his waistband and shoved past me into my cabin. As he moved, he trained it on Ember. She stood frozen, eyes wide, and mouth open. Something inside me snapped and I lunged past him and in front of her.

"No!" I shouted. She clutched the back of my shirt with both hands, and I could sense her terror.

Raptor's heaving chest immediately stopped, and I braced myself for the explosion.

Except it never came. The fucker grinned at me, and my chin pulled back in surprise.

"Somehow I had a feeling," he smugly mused. He tucked his weapon away and slapped a frown back on his mug.

"You have a week and I want George Horacio in our back shed. No more. No less."

"Understood."

He turned to leave and I followed. When we got to the front porch he stopped and glanced over his shoulder at me. "I hope you know what you're doing," he murmured. "And you also better hope she comes around or you're fucked."

"I know," I admitted on a relieved exhale. "And I'm sorry. I had a plan—you know I did. But she… I…."

"You ever try anything like that again and you're done. But I'm not heartless and I can practically smell your mountain lion's restlessly agitation. Which boggles my mind that I never sensed it before, not even an inkling that something was different or special about you like that. How you kept that hidden for so long with the DSMC is a miracle. Anyway, I will back you, but if she's a liability, I will protect my club and my family. Are we clear?" He spoke in low tones so as not to be heard by Ember.

"Crystal."

"She stays in your cabin. I'm not putting her in one of the bunk rooms. I don't know her, so I don't trust her. You have your work cut out for you. Oh, and by the way? The gun wasn't loaded." He walked off and as he passed Gator, Torque, and Phoenix, they stared at me, gave me a chin lift, then followed our president back to the clubhouse.

I wasn't pissed at Phoenix or Torque for ratting me out. They did the right thing. After all, I was supposed to have George Horacio in the back shed right now—like I promised.

Relieved, but still chastising myself, I slumped against

the cabin between the entrance and the window. My head banged back to the wood. What a clusterfuck the night had turned into. The door slowly opened, and I rolled my head to see what she was doing.

With fear in her gaze, she looked up at me.

"Can you promise me you won't hurt me?"

Her request might not have shaken me if she hadn't been trembling head to toe and staring up at me with a wide searching gaze.

"You heard what he said?"

"He was gonna shoot me," she whispered.

"I wasn't gonna let that happen."

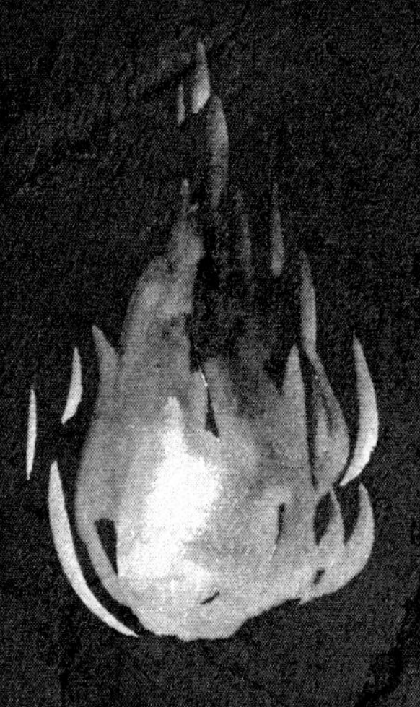

FOUR

Ember

"BAD DAY"—DANIEL POWTER

I don't know why I believed him—the man who had just abducted me. Yet he'd saved me twice in one night. Maybe the first was completely inadvertent, but I couldn't help but feeling I'd rather be stolen by the man in front of me than the one George had promised me to.

"What's your name?" My brow pinched and I tilted my head to study him. He obviously knew a lot about me, but I knew absolutely nothing about him. His crystal-blue gaze was traveling over my body and hell if I couldn't practically feel it.

"They call me Ares," he muttered as he dragged his gaze from where they'd fallen on my chest.

Out of habit, I crossed my arms over my overly large

boobs—at least for my frame. Considering I was all of five-two and my bra size was a 32D. I hated it because it was all everyone noticed. He was obviously no different.

Then he surprised me when he grabbed the bottom of the hoodie he wore. When he lifted it over his head, it raised his dark T-shirt and exposed a small section of firm, sculpted abs that had my jaw dropping. I snapped it shut when he tugged it over his head and tossed it to me. "You look… I mean, you're probably cold."

I caught it and held it close.

It wasn't like I'd planned to go out and about. When I left for George's, I'd dressed in leggings and an old long sleeve Longhorns T-shirt. It was a little thin, but it was soft and comfy—and definitely didn't hide when I was cold. As he sat on the futon, I pulled it over my head. The dark fleece dropped to mid-thigh. It practically swallowed me, but it smelled like crisp outdoors, with a light scent of whatever cologne he wore. Not to mention, it was warm and soft. Absently, I held the cuffs where I peeked my fingers out.

"What do you plan to do with me?" I asked as I sat nervously on the edge of the opposite end from him. The other man had a good point. I could identify Ares and he had no reason to believe I wouldn't. "Do you know who my dad is?"

"Which question do you want me to answer?" he asked with his head resting back and staring at the ceiling. He looked so defeated I found myself feeling a little bad for him—pure insanity.

"Both."

The humorless laugh he snorted made me wish I could hear him really laugh. Which was weird.

"First one? No idea. Second, yeah. I know exactly who your father is."

As I scooted back, I tugged the hoodie over my upraised knees, then rested my chin on my knee. "Then you know he'd pay whatever ransom you wanted. I would tell him I never saw you."

"That's not why I took you," he muttered.

My gaze darted around the small space while I weighed my next words. When it fell back on the handsome man next to me, a shiver skated up my spine. It made me feel strange and like I wished we'd met under different circumstances. Except what he'd done told me we didn't run in the same circles and our paths would've been unlikely to have crossed.

"You said you didn't plan to take me and that you were originally going to kill me. Why?" He'd said George killed his girl. I wasn't sure what he meant by that. The George I'd thought I knew never would've done that, but he already proved to me that I was dead wrong.

"How well do you know your brother?"

"Step-brother," I corrected, snorting at his ability to read my mind.

"Thank God for small favors that you aren't blood related to him," he mumbled, but I still heard him.

"I thought I knew him better than anyone, but tonight he showed me I didn't know him at all." The reality of the evening's events washed over me, and a tear slipped free and tumbled down my cheek. In a romance novel, this would've been the moment when the hero reached over and caught it on his fingertip. Except this was no romance and I had no hero.

"I was part of a group that broke up a—business deal—that he was a part of. He didn't appreciate it and he had his goons open fire on us. Tasha—" he paused, and his nostrils flared. "She was a casualty of that shooting. She died in my arms. I loved her and he took her from me."

What he'd described should've surprised and disgusted me. After tonight the surprise part was non-existent. My heart broke for him.

"I—I can't imagine," I whispered. I was going to say I was sorry, but that seemed an ineffectual platitude. To lose someone you loved like that must have been traumatizing and I could understand his desire for retribution.

"I don't know why I'm even telling you this. The less you know, the better. I'm just one fuck up after another tonight." He sighed and closed his eyes. Then he opened them and rolled his head to the side to look at me. "Which means, now you're my prisoner and I don't know why."

Another tear rolled down my face and I sucked in a startled breath when he reached over and caught it with a calloused finger.

"Fuck, don't cry." Blood rushed through my veins and to my head.

"I'm scared," I softly admitted.

"You should be. Because even if I did ransom you to

your father, that puts you back in danger if what you say is true. From what I know about your brother, I believe he would've sold you to the highest bidder without batting an eye. Then he would've told your father you ran off to Mexico or some shit. If your father didn't believe him, I wouldn't have put it past Horacio to kill him." Him vocalizing my thoughts really drove the reality of my situation home.

"So, I'm stuck here until you um, take care of him?" Talking about someone's pending death in such a casual manner was so alien to me that it was like I was in an alternate dimension.

"Pretty much."

"Oh, okay." I swallowed and stared at my hands as I absently picked at my nails. Chewing on both my lip and what he'd said, I got lost in my head for a moment or two. That's when my brain remembered something crucial and the shock hitting me like a cannonball to the chest.

"I need a favor," I whispered, meeting his penetrating gaze with my worried one.

"What's that?" He cocked a single brow in one of the sexiest moves I'd ever seen.

"You said you could get back into George's house without him knowing?" I scrambled over closer to him and rested on my knees. My hands held my aching heart.

"Yes."

"Mr. Mu is there! You need to go get him. If George could be so callous about human life, he wouldn't hesitate to hurt him. He hates him!" My pulse raced and my stomach churned. I refused to analyze that I was more worried about my cat than about my own safety in my new "prison."

"Who the hell is Mr. Mu?" He looked utterly flabbergasted and in other circumstances, I might've laughed.

"My cat."

His face fell to a deadpan stare. "Your cat?"

"Yes. He's in the room I use at George's. Please," I begged as I gripped his forearm. When my hand wrapped around the corded muscle under smooth, inked skin, I froze. Stuck to his warm flesh as if an electrical current held me there, I couldn't let go.

"I'll see what I can do," he quietly replied as he repeated his earlier motions and tucked my messy hair behind my ear. My breath caught when his fingertips brushed my skin in the process. Then he jerked his hand away from me, as if he'd suddenly caught what he'd been doing.

I leaned back and he cleared his throat. "You can have the bed. I'll sleep here. I'll see if I can get your damn cat."

A smirk came unbidden to my lips. "You kind of suck at this prisoner stuff."

"Christ, don't tell Raptor," he muttered.

"That's the guy who was going to shoot me?" My lungs froze and my heart stuttered at the memory.

"Yes, but I don't think he really would've. I think he was trying to prove a point. It was shitty of him, but I get where he was coming from." He studied a frayed spot on the thigh of his jeans, then looked back at me. "I'm going to do my best to keep you safe. Even though part of you being in danger is because of me."

"Okay," I replied in a near whisper. The man had kidnapped me. Yet, I couldn't seem to find it in me to hate him. Nor was I afraid of him—which was something I was still having a hard time processing.

"Better get some sleep. Bathroom's through there." He pointed as he stood, then walked to the door with cat-like grace and flipped a heavy metal bar over the door. As he turned, he cocked that sexy brow at me again as if daring me to try to get out now. He knew damn well there was no way I could lift the thick slab of metal as easily as he had, and I certainly couldn't be quiet about it if I found a way.

Asshole.

"Windows have alarms—if you were wondering." He slid the futon away from the wall and laid it flat.

Not like I had anywhere to go at the moment. Dad and Rhonda would be out of town for a few weeks. If I went back to my dad's, George could easily get to me. And now? I sure as shit didn't trust him not to try.

Jesus, what was I going to tell my dad? And Rhonda… that was her *son*.

Trying to still all the questions in my head, I used the bathroom. As I washed my hands, I stared at myself in the small mirror. I was a hot mess. Working the band out of my hair, I grimaced when I pulled several strands out with it. Finger-combing it the best I could, I plaited it and banded the end.

Then I returned to the main part of the cabin and stopped short.

Ares was sprawled at an angle on the open futon, one foot hung off and the knuckles of one hand rested on the floor. For a moment, I stood in the quiet cabin and watched the rise and fall of his chest. He twitched and I held my breath, afraid I was about to get caught staring at him like a creeper. Luckily, he took a long deep breath, before settling back into a slow and even pattern.

In sleep, he was beautifully handsome—almost boyishly so. Something about him was compelling, luring me in like there was a mystical wisp of smoke wrapping around me and physically pulling me closer.

My fingers itched to touch him again. The need to feel his warm, smooth skin under my hands, a craving. I found myself wanting to press my lips to that same surface, greedy to taste him.

Yep, it's official. I'm losing my mind. I should be hitting him over the head and escaping.

Shaking off the mesmerizing and bizarre direction of my initial thoughts, I kicked off my Vans and dove into the bed. The mattress was like a cloud and my body quickly relaxed. Except I wasn't used to sleeping in my clothes and I soon became restless.

"Shit," I muttered. Lifting my head, I peeked to ensure Ares was still sleeping. Then I wiggled out of my leggings and panties. I figured I could redress under the covers in the morning, so I rolled them together and shoved them under the spare pillow. I pulled my arms into the hoodie and my T-shirt to slip out of my bra. I stuffed it with the rest.

Sighing in relief, I snugged back into the oversized hoodie and thick blankets. Then I laid there feeling guilty that he was on the futon without a blanket. There was only the top sheet and comforter on the bed, though.

I lifted my head again. Despite the chill in the air, he didn't look cold.

With a huff, I flopped to my side, curled up and surprisingly drifted off to sleep.

FIVE

Ares

"HOLD ME DOWN"—TOMMY LEE

Stiff, I softly groaned and rolled over, then sat up. I rubbed my eyes, then scrubbed my hands through my hair as I yawned. The events of the last twenty-four hours came back to me, and I immediately checked the door, finding it secure. Then I looked over at my bed.

What I saw caused me to suck in a sharp breath through my teeth. Inside, my mountain lion grew restless. A rumble started in my chest, and I fought the voice that screamed in my head.

Christ.

Silently, I got to my feet and padded to the edge of the

mattress. Laying on her stomach, she had kicked off the covers. My hoodie had ridden up, exposing the bottom of her very bare and perfectly-rounded ass cheeks. Golden hair in a braided rope wrapped around her to rest under her chin. Full pink lips, parted slightly in sleep, quivered, then stilled. As I reached for the covers to place them back over her, she cocked one leg up and I caught a flash of wet pink that sent my already problematic morning wood, into a full-on boner.

"Fucking hell," I whispered. Before I could do something really stupid, like run a finger through that slick pink slit, I gingerly picked up the covers and settled them over her. Inside, my mountain lion grew restless. A rumble started in my chest. I wanted to rip my clothes off and climb in the bed with her. A vision flashed through my mind of me sinking my teeth into her flesh as I drove into her.

It had me stumbling back.

Since the day Tasha had died, my sex drive had been pretty non-existent. There were more than enough fingers on one hand to count the number of times I'd been with a woman since. With plenty left over. I shouldn't be reacting to her like I was. Besides, I hadn't been good enough for Tasha and I sure as hell wouldn't ever be good enough for this woman.

While I knew she was sleeping, I took a quick—cold—shower and wrapped a towel around my waist. Sticking my head out to ensure she was still asleep, I snuck out and over to the closet. Then I dropped the towel, pulled on a clean pair of jeans and grabbed a T-shirt. I turned to go to my nightstand where I kept my socks, to find wide blue eyes staring at me over the top of the comforter.

"Enjoying the view?" I asked while I casually tugged the shirt over my head. Inside, my heart was racing as my stomach tightened and rippled as a bunch of iron-winged butterflies banged around. It was an unwelcome feeling that left me surly. Especially since I'd certainly enjoyed the view she'd presented earlier. With a frown, I zipped and fastened my pants.

"It's not like you were being modest about it," she replied in a voice muffled by the covers.

I snorted. "You were sleeping—it's not like I was showing off. You can shower if you want."

Then I shuffled into the kitchen. Sticking to the thoughts in my head and ignoring the temptress behind me, I gathered what I needed to make pancakes. In my peripheral, I caught a flash of shapely legs as she rushed into the bathroom. I shook my head and returned to my task at hand. In no time, I had whipped up a stack for her and one for myself.

She came out wearing the same clothes from yesterday and guilt hit me again. From the way my hoodie swallowed her whole, I knew that none of my other clothes were an option for her. If she was gonna stay here, I needed to get her something to wear. Motioning to the bar, I set the plates down and grabbed butter and syrup from my fridge.

"I have to go to the clubhouse to talk to Raptor. Can I trust you to stay here?" I asked as I sat on one stool and prepared my food. By the time I shoveled the first bite into my mouth, she still hadn't answered, nor had she sat down to eat. A glance over toward her showed her nervously chewing on her lip. "You don't like pancakes?"

"I do."

"Then eat. They're getting cold." I pointed my fork at her plate.

She tried to move the stool over without being obvious and I understood the issue. Though I had nothing on Raptor, I wasn't a really small guy, and I was crowding her space. Even with the distance she created, her elbow brushed mine. The zing I experienced despite the layer of fleece that separated us, had me pausing with my hand halfway to my mouth.

"I need your word that you'll stay in the cabin. If I can't trust you to do that, then I have no choice than to cuff you to the bed." I had two things to take care of today that simply couldn't wait.

After a wide-eyed start, she nodded. The still damp hair she had piled on top of her head wobbled and a few golden strands fell free.

"Trust me when I tell you, you don't want to be out there alone. Not until we know your brother—"

"He's not my brother," she cut in with a snarl. Damn, she was sexy when she was angry.

"Fair. Not until we know *George* isn't a threat anymore."

We ate in silence for several bites, then she set down her fork. She stared at her plate. "What are you going to do to him?"

"It's probably best you don't know that," I muttered. Trying to reduce her culpability was a losing battle. The less she knew, the better. The problem with that rationale was she knew what we looked like and what I'd said to George. In other words, I was already fucked.

"When will you be back?" she quietly asked between

bites. Though she seemed subdued, I appreciated that she wasn't afraid of me. Despite what I'd put her through—well, George had a hand in her mental trauma from the day before, too—she didn't cower.

"Dunno. There's food in the fridge and the cabinets. Help yourself to whatever you want." After inhaling my food, I got up and rinsed my dishes. "I'll do these when I get back."

Before I went outside, I opened my small biometric safe and withdrew the two guns I kept in there. Thankfully, the brothers had grabbed my Micro 9 after I unexpectedly shifted the night at Raptor's ex's place. Ensuring the clip was fully loaded, I tucked it in the inside pocket of my cut. The second was a small Sig Sauer.

The metal bar scraped on the brackets as I lifted it and set it to the side. When I turned the knob, I cast a glance over my shoulder. What I saw did something weird to my insides. Ember sat at the bar, chin resting on her hand with her elbow on the counter as she stared out the window at the gloomy morning. Soft blonde wisps waved around her face and thick dark lashes feathered the tops of her cheeks when she closed her eyes and took a deep breath. In profile, she looked ethereal.

Fighting the inexplicable pull, I balled up my hands and left.

When I got to the chapel, I took my seat next to Phoenix and waited for everyone else.

"How's the prisoner?" he asked with a smirk. He casually slouched in the chair as he gave me his full attention.

I shot him a glare. "She's not my prisoner. I mean, not really."

He snorted. "Can she leave?"

"No."

"Then she's a prisoner."

"Not true. Right now, it's just not safe for her to leave."

"Whatever helps you sleep at night."

"Shut the fuck up." I leaned my elbows on the tabletop and buried my face in my hands.

His chuckle was soon covered by the booted footsteps of our brothers as they entered the room. I sat back and waited as Gator, One Short, and Torque came in.

"Any news on Tigger's family?" I asked One Short when he sat across from me.

He and Gator looked somber. One Short shook his head. Turned out that when the prick tased him, he whacked his head on the stone steps. Raptor's dad assessed him, but we ended up taking him to the hospital where he'd been been rushed into surgery. He had fractured his skull, causing an aneurysm that they were unable to repair. He was pronounced before any of us got a chance to see him again. We'd been trying to track down his family, but they'd moved several times and the last time, didn't leave a forwarding address.

"Fuck. That means, they don't even know he's gone." It sucked because he was a fit, healthy guy and then suddenly, he was gone. We all knew that with this life it could happen to any of us, but that didn't make it easier to process.

"No, but it doesn't seem like they were close. I mean, like at all." One Short slowly shook his head.

Raptor walked in and we all glanced his way. My brows hit my hairline and he stabbed a finger at me. "Shut it."

"I didn't say anything," I argued holding my hands up in a mock plea for mercy.

Our president gingerly sat with his newborn daughter sleeping in a sling-looking contraption on his chest. Despite recent events and the reason for this meeting, it took everything I had not to chuckle.

The sling was hot pink.

And little Shae looked tiny as fuck compared to his massive frame.

Gator pulled his lips between his teeth and Raptor gave him a narrowed-eyed stare.

"Sage is exhausted. This is the only way Shae will sleep right now and they both need some rest," he quietly explained, then motioned toward me. "Tell him."

Gator sighed. "Horacio skipped town."

"Fuck," I muttered as I briefly closed my eyes.

"It gets worse," Raptor warned.

With my stomach cramping, I waited to hear what Gator had to say.

"They're looking for the chick—and you. Facet intercepted a wanted ad on the dark web." Gator held my gaze.

"Her name is Ember, not *the chick*," I grumbled as I palmed my face, then let my hand fall to the table. Five sets of eyes locked on me, and I grew defensive. "What?"

"What do you plan to do now?" Gator slowly questioned.

"George was basically going to sell her. I can't let him get to her."

One Short cocked a brow and Phoenix sat there grinning at me. What a fucker.

"Dude was gonna sell his own sister?" Torque drawled in disbelief.

"Yeah, that's what she said," I replied with a sigh.

"You believe her?" Raptor quietly asked me.

"I do."

"What about you? If they're looking for you, they're gonna find us too. That puts our families in danger." Gator crossed him arms and scowled.

"Ares is one of us. We protect our own," Raptor firmly chimed in, then looked my way. "Despite their stupid decisions."

I opened my mouth to argue, but he held up a hand to silence me. "You went against the plan, not because you were forced to adjust fire, but because you 'changed your mind.' That was stupid. I'm not saying I don't understand your rationale, because I get it. 100%. But I also noticed you were extremely protective of her."

"So?" I swallowed hard because talking about the bizarre effect she had on me made me uncomfortable as hell.

"Soooo, if you were… oh, I don't know… claiming her… that would make her family as well." Raptor gave me a pointed look.

It made me fidgety and my skin itched. It was like being a kid in the principal's office.

"I don't know her," I argued though my mountain lion stirred.

"You don't need to if she's your mate," he calmly replied.

The big cat in me screamed *yes, mine!*

And it shook me to the core.

"I need to get into George's house," I mumbled.

"What the fuck for? He ain't there!" One Short stared at me like I was nuts.

I palmed my face and dragged my hands down before I admitted, "I need to go get her cat."

You could've heard a pin drop before they all burst out laughing and Shae started to cry.

"Goddammit!" Raptor groaned.

According to the cameras at George's place, no one was in the house except for the housekeeper. Since that was the case, I slapped a set of fake plates on my truck and drove it. I'd have rather ridden my bike, but there was no way in hell I was getting a cat and all its shit on my bike.

Facet had looked into it, and there were no missing person reports, and there were certainly no public outcries for the return of Simon Cole's daughter. Which meant George hadn't said a word. It wasn't like I needed to hide my face—he'd already seen it. Still, I looped the cameras when I stopped in front of the house.

Deciding to play it off, I'd dressed in my nicest clothes. Checking out my appearance in the sidelight of the door, I acknowledged that I cleaned up pretty nice. Then I rang the doorbell.

An older woman answered the door. Expression wary, she peeked around the door she held in a white-knuckle grip. In heavily accented English, she asked, "Can I help you?"

"Hi, I'm a friend of Ember's. She ended up going on the cruise with her parents since George was leaving and she asked me to swing by and pick up her cat."

"Gato?" She tilted her head in confusion.

I repeated myself in fluent Spanish. It had come in handy with the migrant workers we had up in Minnesota over the summers. After making friends with a few of the kids that had been with their parents, I'd quickly picked it up.

A wide grin lit her wrinkled face as she introduced herself as Elena. "I didn't know she had brought the prince," she rattled off in Spanish. "If I'd known, I would've taken care of him."

"That's kind of you, and she said you probably would, but she didn't want to risk him making a mess or breaking something that would anger her brother." I gave her my best smile and her cheeks grew rosy. She seemed like a nice lady, and it made me wonder what the fuck she was doing working for George Horacio.

She motioned for me to follow, and I trailed her up the stairs.

"Where are you from originally?" I asked her, making small talk, though I knew she was born in South America. It listed her arrival in the U.S. when she was younger. Her employment was obviously under the table as she had no record of income. That hadn't surprised me, because I knew a lot of people who immigrated from South America sent the majority of what they made back to family.

Her spine went ramrod straight and she cast a nervous glance at me. "Venezuela."

By her tone, I guessed that was a topic that wasn't up for discussion. If her fear was me turning her in, I was no threat. I tried to give her a reassuring smile. Something seemed off, and I made a mental note to look into Elena deeper. There hadn't been much information on her in the file I'd gotten from Raptor. It hadn't even said she was mostly Spanish speaking. Just that she wasn't a security risk.

We stopped at the last door on the west side of the upstairs. She opened the door, and a plaintive meow came from under the bed.

"He's upset," she cooed as she got to her knees and peeped under the bed. I rolled my eyes behind her back. It was a fucking house cat. While she tried, I glanced around the room. Other than the small suitcase in the corner, there was very little there that personalized the room.

Despite her attempts, she couldn't coax him out. My arms were long enough, and I figured I could reach him. Repeating her actions, I got down on my knees. Under the middle of the bed, he crouched, staring at me. His blue eyes narrowed, and he hissed at me.

"Great," I muttered. I slowly reached for him, but he took off out the other side. When he darted around the foot of the bed, I lunged and caught him. He growled and grumbled. My inner cat returned the sentiment, but I kept both of them under control.

Thankfully, Elena helped me pack up the cat's crap. The damn thing had its own bag. There were two unused disposable litter boxes propped behind the door.

"She wanted me to grab the things she left here so she

could get them when she picks up Mu," I kindly explained to the helpful housekeeper. "One stop on her way home and all."

"Of course!" She helped me gather the few items in the bathroom and put it in the suitcase that was still mostly packed.

She prattled on about hoping the "young miss" enjoyed the trip and how she was glad she went, as I trailed her downstairs. The entire way, the heavy as fuck cat made a low growling noise and bared its teeth at me.

"Knock it off you little fucker, or I'm leaving you here," I thought. The cat immediately stopped, but seemed to continue glaring at me.

This was going to be a nightmare.

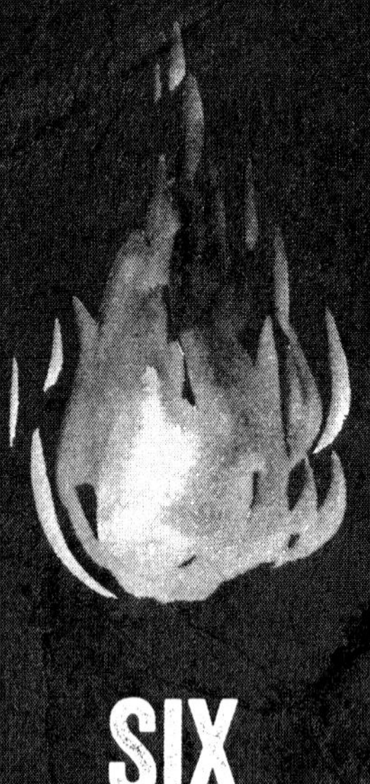

SIX

Ember

"TAKE ME DOWN"—THE PRETTY RECKLESS

"Are you fucking kidding me?" I heard through the fog of sleep. With a grumble, I turned over and blinked my eyes to adjust to the light shining from the bathroom.

"Wassamatta?" I mumbled. I'd been sleeping like a baby in the man's cabin for three days now. During the day I was starting to go a little stir crazy, but at night? At night I crashed. Maybe it was the bed.

There were several sounds that I'd have sworn were an argument, followed by rustling. Then Ares came out of the bathroom carrying Mr. Mu by the scruff and supporting his weight with the other hand. Mushu looked furious.

"He shredded my fucking underwear again!" A deep scowl darkened his features and I had to pull the pillow up over my face to hide my smile. Because despite his anger he was gorgeous, and it was hilarious to me that Mr. Mu had been ripping up the crotch of every pair of underwear he came across.

If I didn't know better, I would've thought he growled at Mu.

"He's just a cat, he doesn't know what he's doing," I replied, doing my best to keep a straight face.

"Just a cat?" he asked with bugged eyes and a gaping mouth. "This thing easily weighs forty pounds! He's huge and he hates me. I saved his ass from abandonment, and this is the thanks I get?"

Over the last several days, Ares and I had fallen into a companionable, though tenuous… relationship? Friendship? I had no idea what else to call what we had going on. The sexual tension was off the charts. I didn't quite know what to do with that, but goodness, the man was hot. I'd never been able to erase the sculpted abs and holy fuck… that ass… from my mind. That first day when he'd dropped his towel to dress, I'd about died. He might've thought I was sleeping, but if I was, I was dreaming.

"This demon feline hates me," he snapped. Mushu growled at him, then hissed, and I lost it. "You think this is funny? He has a personal vendetta against me!"

"You stole his mama," I told him with a shrug.

With a glare to me, then my cat, he marched over and

ceremoniously dropped him in my lap. "He does it again? He's going outside."

Mr. Mu growled at him, and I stroked his head in a soothing manner. "Shhh. The big bad man won't kick you out," I crooned. "He shouldn't leave his dirty clothes all over the floor, should he?"

Ares's nostrils flared and his eyes narrowed to grouchy slits. His fingers flexed several times, and he inhaled deeply before letting it out slowly. "He has no idea what a 'big bad man' I am. But he's about to if he keeps it up."

I stuck out my bottom lip and shot him puppy dog eyes. But in my head, I screamed, *"Yes! I wanna see what a big bad man you are!"*

"Don't," he demanded as he pointed his finger at me. Him ordering me about shouldn't be a turn on, but hell if I didn't have to clench my thighs together. It was crazy, but it was almost as if he knew—like he could sense it. Because his striking icy gaze heated and fell to my lap. Except any time he seemed to be attracted to me, it appeared to piss him off. This time was no different. He spun on his heel and stomped to the front door and jerked it open.

"When you're dressed, leave that asshole here and come down to the clubhouse." Without waiting for a reply or to see my unhinged jaw, he left. The slam of the door echoed in the silence.

I looked down into eyes that seemed eerily similar to the man who had just stormed out. "Why did you do that?" I whispered to him. He wiggled and struggled until he was out of my arms. He pranced to the edge of the bed where he settled regally and blinked at me with his judgey hooded gaze.

"Now what the hell am I being summoned to the castle for?" I asked Mu. The entire time I'd been here, no one came to the cabin but Ares—and I hadn't left. It made me nervous. But then if it was bad, surely they wouldn't allow me to walk there unescorted.

Right?

I dressed in a pair of leggings and a Santa Cruz hoodie, then slipped my feet in my Vans and braided my hair. There wasn't a reason to get dolled up, so I skipped makeup.

"Be a good boy," I sternly admonished Mushu before I kissed his velvety soft head. Then I left the cabin for the first time in days. For a moment, I stood on the porch and breathed deeply. The crisp air filled my lungs as I glanced around. Six cabins, one larger than the rest, sat in a semicircle. The front porches all faced the larger metal building that Ares had pointed out as the "clubhouse." Several guys stood out behind the building smoking and each one watched me closely.

"Well, that explains why you weren't afraid to let me go out by myself," I quietly muttered.

Unsure if I should take the front or back door, I decided to pull up my big girl britches and headed toward the men. It didn't matter that my heart was beating up into my throat or that I had the shakes something fierce. To hide the tremble of my hands, I tucked them into my hoodie pocket and set out.

I hadn't gone far when I caught a whiff and knew it wasn't cigarettes they were smoking. The guy with iced blond tips on his hair stared down his nose at me as he took a deep drag.

"Now I see why he kept you and didn't wanna let you go," he said, but his lips didn't move from where they were around the joint. Don't ask how I knew neither of the other guys had said it. He blew out a cloud of smoke and waited as I approached.

Scared, but not wanting to show it, I marched right up to him and stopped when I was nearly toe-to-toe with him. Then I reached up and plucked the joint from his fingertips and took a hit. The flash of surprise in his dark blue gaze almost made me laugh. I almost did as I coughed slightly from the initial shock of the heated smoke hitting the back of my throat.

"Oh, yeah. Totally see it, now." And a chuckle. That time I was positive his mouth didn't move. And though I swear he spoke directly into my head, I hadn't been imagining things and I wasn't losing my damn mind. I took a second smaller hit then handed it back. The entire time I stared him down, noting all the ink that ran up his neck from under his jacket.

As he held back a grin, he handed the last of the joint off to an older guy. That guy looked me up and down.

"How old are you? Are you even legal?" he asked with a chuckle.

"How old are *you?*" I glanced to the magician, ventriloquist, or whatever the fuck he was and smirked. "Someone needs to call the nursing home and find out where he left his wheelchair, then come get him."

It was a bold move and one that had me inwardly second guessing. This could end so badly. Why hadn't I ever learned to keep my mouth shut?

The blond guy and the third dude, cracked up laughing. The older guy scowled and snorted.

"Come on, I'll take you inside," the blond offered. "Follow me."

As I passed the older guy, I winked at him. The scowl lifted and the corner of his mouth kicked up. The third man who had remained silent followed us.

The heavy metal door slammed as we passed into the blessed warmth of the interior. No way would I have admitted I was freezing out there.

"So, what's your name?" I asked.

"Blade," he replied.

"That's what they call you. Right?"

He glanced my way with a questioning tilt of his head.

"You guys all have these names that people call you. But surely your mom didn't name you Blade," I explained.

He paused. "No. No, she didn't. But no matter how much I like your spunk, I don't know you and I'm not telling you a damn thing."

It wasn't said hatefully, but I was left feeling like a deflated balloon. My bravado had run out, which sucked. Because that left me feeling weak and vulnerable. Two things I despised.

With my life as I knew it, falling apart, I was

adrift—hanging on to a tiny, rotting log that barely kept me afloat.

We resumed our trek, and he led me to a room that kind of reminded me of a small conference room. Then he motioned to a chair against the wall. Warily, I took a seat while several men filed into the room. The guy that pointed a gun at me that first night came in and my spine stiffened. Prepared to flee, I was vigilant and on edge. The last one in was Ares, who shut the door. He made eye contact with me for all of about two seconds before he sat at the table.

The man from the first night sat in the seat at the head of the table. He gave me a curt nod. Then he introduced himself as Raptor, the president of the chapter, and everyone around the table introduced themselves afterward. I learned that the guy who had silently followed us in was Phoenix.

"Miss Cole," Raptor began once they'd all finished.

"Yes… your honor?" I hesitantly replied.

His lips twisted as he seemed to fight a grin. When he got himself composed, he corrected me. "Just call me Raptor."

"Right," I muttered as my cheeks flamed. How embarrassing, but in my defense, this world was nothing like the one I normally lived in.

"I apologize for how you ended up here," Raptor started with. "I also apologize for how we met."

Unsure if I was supposed to talk, I nodded.

"Something you should understand is that I'm very

protective of my family and my club. I'm also protective of the families of my brothers."

Confused, I skirted my gaze around the room, trying to gauge the mood and what was going on. Again, I nodded as I nervously swirled the end of my braid around my finger.

"Ares told me about what transpired before he walked into your brother's office. That type of thing isn't tolerated with us. It's part of the reason we have beef with your brother."

"Um, sir, he's *not* my brother," I blurted out. "And if you know what happened, then you know I have 'beef' with him too."

"Fair enough. The reason you're here for this meeting is because I need your word that you can keep your mouth shut about us if we let you go." He stared at me so intently, I squirmed in my seat.

"Like I told Ares that first night, he inadvertently saved me. He could've followed through with what he said he was going to do, but he didn't. By taking me from George's home, he saved me from God knows what."

"No, we know too. It's not just God," the older guy from outside, One Short, muttered.

"You know what was going to happen to me? How? You weren't there," I said.

The man met my gaze with a look that seemed almost apologetic. "Because we know the things he's involved in."

"Trust me when I tell you, it's better you don't know the extent of your—George's—dealings. What you need to know is that we plan to be the end of George," Raptor continued. The way he watched me, I half wondered if he could read my mind. He was a super intense guy.

"And by that you mean, you're going to kill him," I clarified with a sour stomach.

"Yes," Raptor bluntly replied. I started a bit at his blunt honesty.

"And if I open my mouth, then I join him… is that what you're trying to allude to? Because I'd rather you just come out and say things. My dad raised me to be tougher than you give me credit for. So don't sugar coat things," I insisted. My hairs stood on end, and I was nearly choking on my heart that was suddenly sitting in my throat. Still, I boldly held his stare. I would not show weakness.

"If necessary, then yes. I will eliminate any and all threats to those that are important to me," he explained.

"I'm not going to tell anyone a damn thing," I promised, as my head spun.

"And do you understand that for your own safety, you need to stay here and out of sight until we have accomplished our objective?" Gator asked. When he spoke, I moved my attention to the vice president.

"Yes, sir."

"Then you have permission to come and go from Ares's cabin to the clubhouse. You can walk the property with two exceptions." Raptor chimed in.

"Okay?" I wet my lips nervously and wiped my sweaty palms on my thighs.

"You stay away from the fence lines and the back of

the property. There are two hundred acres here. There are yellow ribbons on the trees that delineate the end of the area you're free to explore. Tonight, we're having a get together with our friends and family. If you want to join us, you're welcome. For as long as you obey the rules, you are here as our guest. Give me one reason to doubt your sincerity and all bets are off. Understood?" He lifted his brow and shot me a questioning look.

"Yes. Absolutely."

"Then we'll see you tonight." That felt like my cue to leave, so I started to stand, but worried I was being presumptuous, paused partway out of my chair.

"Yes, you can go. Keenan is at the bar right now if you want something to drink," Raptor offered. "Sage will be over after she gets our daughter fed."

"And my ol' lady will be here shortly. Her name is Sloane and she'll probably have her crazy but loyal friend Niara with her," Phoenix added. Jesus, the men in this group were insanely gorgeous. Even One Short appeared to have been very handsome in his youth. Wherever the signup for them was, I wanted to be on the selection board. Or whatever they called it.

Relief washed over me, and I got to my feet. I paused at the door, then bravely glanced at the man in charge. "I have one favor."

He cocked a brow and waited.

Swallowing my unease, I took a deep breath and let it out in a whoosh. "It needs to look like an accident. His mom is going to be devastated as it is. I don't want her finding out about any of this. She's a good person who has been a good wife to my dad and a good mom to me in the absence of my own."

My gaze found Ares's to find him watching me. For a moment, the room disappeared, and I was lost in the ocean of those blue, blue eyes. A clearing throat snapped me out of it, and I quickly tacked on a "please," then scurried out of the room.

Once I went out in the main part of the building, I wandered around, checking things out. On the walls were neon lights like you might find in a bar, but there were also framed photographs. I peered at unfamiliar faces, but it was hard not to get caught up in the moment of the image. With the exception of a few, they were all smiling or laughing. Arms slung around each other, they posed for the camera. There were even a couple that were in black and white.

"That's one of the founding members," a familiar voice said from behind me, and I practically jumped out of my skin. When I spun, I did a double take. I stared at the man in front of me, then toward the room I'd just left. The door hadn't opened, but Phoenix was there.

"You—in there—here—what the hell?" I was unable to make a complete sentence, I was so confused.

He chuckled and I realized his hair was a little shorter and he wasn't wearing a cut.

"I'm Keenan. From your reaction, I'm guessing you didn't know Phoenix and I are twins." His grin was brilliant and damn near mesmerizing. "Would you like me to make you a drink?"

"It's like nine in the morning," I replied with a confused frown.

His laughter rang out and I found myself grinning. It was an infectious sound. "Trust me when I tell you, I don't think these guys care," he murmured conspiratorially.

When he went behind the bar, I took a seat on one of the stools in front of him.

"So, are you like an employee here?"

"No, not exactly," he replied. "You want something?"

"Umm, just a Diet Coke?"

"Of course." He grabbed a glass and started filling it with ice. While he made the drink, I looked around. From the outside, the building seemed relatively small, but it was obviously bigger than it seemed.

Where I was sitting was an L-shaped bar that seemed to have access to a kitchen of sorts in the corner. To my right was a small stage with what I was pretty sure was a freaking stripper pole. Next to that, there was a couch, then in the center were several tables. There was a pool table and a small bar-like area by the side door that I assumed was where they checked people in if they came for a party or whatever.

All in all, it had a cool vibe.

He set the glass in front of me and leaned on his elbows, bringing him close enough that I caught a hint of his aftershave. It was a clean, fresh scent. We made small talk for a while and he told me about how he was originally from Chicago, but had moved to Iowa as a teen.

Sunlight flooded the dimly lit room when three

women, one carrying a baby, came in. There was a redhead, a brunette with the baby, and the third woman had long jet-black hair and carried a folded-up bassinet. They stopped short for a moment when they saw me, and I braced myself for an attack. Because they didn't look happy.

"Hello, ladies," Keenan called out and they came over to the bar. The black-haired one and the brunette went into the kitchen and came out empty-handed, so I assumed they set up the baby bed and put the baby down to nap.

"Who are you?" The redhead looked me up and down as she waited for my reply.

"Niara! Don't be so rude!" The black-haired woman hissed.

"She's okay. I'm Ember Cole," I offered as I held out a hand.

Hearing my name changed everything. All three women lost their wary expressions and smiled. I learned that Sloane was the one with black hair who was with Phoenix. Niara was her friend, and Sage was the brunette with the baby, and Raptor's fiancée. Shae was the baby, but she was sleeping, and I didn't want to risk waking her up.

Not that I would tell any of them, but babies kind of scared me. I'd never been around them much growing up since all of my younger "cousins" were around my age.

"We thought for a minute that you were one of those *club girls*," Niara told me with a sneer.

"Oh," I replied, not really sure what that meant but assuming it was similar to buckle bunnies at rodeos or a puck bunny at a hockey game. Keenan chuckled at her as he leaned on his elbows across from me.

The sound of a door opening preceded the sound of boots on concrete. The men from the conference room poured out into the room. Ares's gaze immediately found me, and a scowl darkened his face. Keenan stood up.

"Interesting," Sage murmured.

"What?" I asked, though I was still looking at Ares as he approached.

"Mmm, nothing. Feeling a little deja vu Just gonna wait to see what happens," she vaguely replied.

"I need to talk to you," Ares said when he stopped next to me.

With my body reacting to his proximity, I got to my feet.

SEVEN

Ares

"REDEMPTION"—THREE DAYS GRACE

Before I could leave the room, Raptor and Gator stopped me.

"Yeah?" I asked, trying not to sound as irritable as I was. Being in such close proximity to Ember every night and waking up to her hair splayed across my pillow each morning was driving me nuts.

"We think you need to work Ember a little," Raptor replied as he stood there with his arms crossed. Gator leaned a shoulder against the wall and assumed a similar pose.

"Excuse me?" Surely, they weren't suggesting what I thought they were.

"Jesus, Raptor, you're getting soft now that you got a family. What our P is trying to tactfully say is you need to get her to fall for you. You know… the whole wine and dine shit," Gator said with a smirk.

"Wait. Are you telling me to fuck her and manipulate her?" My blood was starting to boil.

"No. I'm telling you to earn her trust. Ensure she will keep her mouth closed like she promised. You know I don't hurt women and children, but if it's her or my family, I will choose my family every time," Raptor sternly explained. "And you will be the one who has to clean up this mess."

"So, manipulate her and make her fall for me," I reiterated. My brain was screaming in outrage, but my goddamn dick was perking up and taking notice. My heart was still black and broken so it wasn't in the game.

"You make it sound so crass." Gator chuckled as if this was all a big joke. "She's a pretty girl. You obviously like her or you would've had her in one of the bunk rooms instead of your cabin."

My eyes went wide. "Whoa. Wait. Uh-uh. Prez told me if she was staying here, she had to be in my cabin. That if we had other brothers come to stay, we wouldn't want her exposed to them."

Gator cocked his brow and turned his smirk to Raptor who rubbed the back of his neck and seemed to wince as he looked down.

"You guys are fucked up," I told them and walked away. I heard their snappy whispers behind me. Then I caught up to Torque and Blade who had stopped to talk and continued out to the common area with them.

What I saw out there sent my blood boiling again. Keenan. All up close and personal smiling at Ember from across the bar. They were so close their hands were almost touching.

I saw red.

It barely registered with me that Sage was watching us with a knowing grin. All I knew was my feet carried me into her airspace where to stopped.

"I need to talk to you," I muttered. She stood up and I assumed she'd follow. I needed to get the hell out of the clubhouse.

Full or irritation, I stormed back to my cabin.

"Oh my God! Slow down!" she huffed and puffed from behind me.

I stopped dead in my tracks and turned to wait for her. She slowed in front of me and braced her hands on her knees as she bent over. In my mind's eye, I saw my hands gripping her hips and driving my cock deep inside her.

Fucking hell.

"My legs are a lot shorter than yours, you know," she panted. "Sweet baby Jesus, I'm out of shape."

Her shape looked perfect to me, but hell if I said that. If I hadn't been having inappropriate fantasies about my unexpected roommate for the last several days, before, thanks to Raptor and Gator, I was now.

And that was the last thing I wanted. I swore I would never want anything more than a hot sweaty night in the dark from a woman ever again. Me having constant images of the things I wanted to do with the little blonde sprite running through my head wasn't supporting that promise to myself.

"What's the big rush? And what's the emergency that I had to go right now?" she demanded in a tone heavy with exasperation.

"Don't worry, I won't keep you long and you can go back to *Keenan*." I hated that I sneered and drew out Keenan's name.

"What?" Shock was written all over her face and I had to reel myself in.

Jesus, why was I acting like this? And why did the slight flare of her perfect nose and the little puffs of steam that escaped from her parted lips turn me on?

"Nothing," I muttered as I pinched the bridge of my nose. Maybe Raptor was right when he told me it wasn't healthy to keep my mountain lion suppressed. After I talked to her, I was going to try to release my frustrations.

When she wrapped her arms around herself and shivered, I motioned for her to go inside with me.

Once the door was closed and the warmth enveloped us, I ran a frustrated hand through my hair.

"I'm sorry. I'm being a dick to you, and you don't deserve it. I'm just catching a lot of shit for my actions the night I took you. I know it was a stupid decision, but I still feel it was the right one. I'm going to try to get this wrapped up as soon as I can, so you can get back to your life. By bringing you here, I both saved you and put you in the biggest danger of your life." Then I pressed my lips together and squeezed my eyes shut for a moment.

When I opened them again, I sent her a pleading stare. "If you don't follow through with what you promised, it will be me that has to make it right."

"You'd have to kill me?" The horrified look on her face made my stomach cramp. I didn't like the idea of her being afraid of me, but it was probably for the best.

"Yes."

"Oh."

"Yeah, oh." The thought of being the one to snuff the life from her nearly drove me mad. My brain was practically short circuiting and my chest ached so bad I could barely breathe.

We stood there in silence for a moment before she broke eye contact and went to the bathroom. The second she shut the door I heard a growl. I found fucking Mushu sitting on the corner of the bed, blue eyes narrowed as he stared a hole in me. A rumble started in my chest, and I thought, "*Don't push me.*"

His eyes flared, then he laid down and appeared to go to sleep.

Needing to get out of there before I crawled out of my skin, I slipped outside. Then with determined strides, I made my way back to the opening in the fence. Sure, I could've gone out the front, but I didn't want to answer questions, nor did I want to be seen at the moment.

With each step I took I thought about the days to come. What I would need to do when George Horacio got back, or we could pinpoint him in one location long enough to go get him. If only we could get a hold of whoever he had covering his tracks. Because they were damn good. Facet was having a hard time cracking the guy's code and getting a lock on George's whereabouts. Every time Facet found him, it was too late, and George had already left.

Then I thought about taking Ember back home.

Why did it feel like my life would be torn apart again? I'd known her less than a week. It was insanity talking. It had to be, because this—these feelings—they weren't me.

Once I reached the spot, I stood out of view of the camera watching the opening. Then, I stripped off my clothes, ignoring the cold, and braced myself for the agonizing jolt that would rip through me as I shifted. A screaming snarl ripped from my open mouth, and I knew it had happened flawlessly, if only it could be as painless.

Restless energy held me in its grip and I flexed muscles I hadn't used in over a week, if not two. Then I nosed through the fence and took off at a lope. By now, I knew the area. I knew where I could run and where I needed to stay hidden. There was still some ranch land around us, which was nice. I didn't know what I'd do if the day came where they developed all around us. To be limited to two hundred acres seemed like a prison to the sleek and powerful cat I was bound to.

We need her. The cat grumbled.

Jesus, shut up. We are not a "we"—we're one and the same.

In a matter of speaking. And you just said we.

Reaching a rise, I slowed and after prowling for the perfect spot, I dropped to the ground. Though it was cold, the sun warmed me. Feeling more at peace than I had in ages, I lowered my lids and basked in the silence. The chaotic feelings and thoughts were gone.

What wasn't gone was the burning need to sink between Ember's thighs and never come up for air.

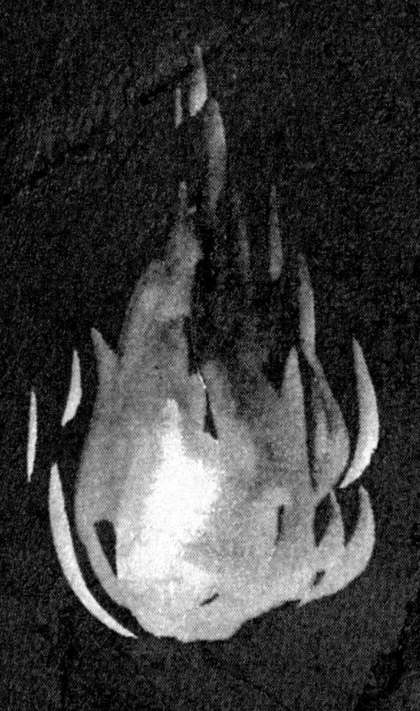

EIGHT

Ember

"BROUGHT TO LIGHT"—GEMINI SYNDROME

When I came out of the bathroom, he was gone. Sitting by the window, I watched and waited for him to come back. The entire time, I tried to make sense of how I was feeling. If I was completely transparent with myself, I was in a compound of criminals.

The right thing to do when I finally got out of here, would be to go to the law. Yet, the thought of Ares being locked up and never seeing him again tore me apart. Not to mention the others. The brief interactions with the people here left me feeling a certain bond with them.

Why?

Was it because they were essentially protecting me?

Without answers, my shoulders slumped. Mushu meowed up at me from where I was absently stroking him as he lay across my lap.

"Where did he go?" If my cat could roll his eyes, I swear he would've at my question. "Why do you really dislike him so much?"

Unable to answer my rhetorical question he gave me a chirping purr and closed his eyes.

The sun began to set, and I noticed people gathering behind the clubhouse where Blade, Phoenix, and One Short had been standing earlier. There was a fire pit they were starting up and the smallest of flickering flames were visible over the edge.

After taking one last glance in the distance and another to the road that I figured led to the front gate, I sighed and got up to join everyone outside. I wasn't sure I was going to be much for company, but I couldn't stand staying in the cabin alone another minute.

Flipping my hood up, I went outside and tucked my hands in the pocket. Hesitating on the edge of the small deck, I scanned the horizon again. In the waning golden hues, I watched for the shape of a man returning.

Disappointed, I chewed on my lip, then headed over to the fire.

I was a little unsettled to see a chick with purple hair and huge tits spilling out of the tight Henley she wore mostly unbuttoned. She sat in Gator's lap and teased along his beard with a talon-like nail. This life may be foreign to me, but I was pretty sure she was one of those "club girls" Niara was talking about.

Then I saw where the women were chatting amicably in lawn chairs on the other side of the now blazing fire. Skirting around the hussy fawning on Gator, I made my way back to them.

"Ember!" Niara called out. "Come sit with us, Chica!"

Chuckling, I decided I liked the outspoken redhead already. Once I reached them, I saw that not only Sage held a baby, so did Sloane. Hers was obviously older, but cute as a bug's ear. "She's adorable," I murmured as I leaned over to smile at her.

"Thank you. I'm biased, but I think so." Sloane giggled.

"That's cuz she looks like her auntie Neenee. Doesn't she?" Niara cooed to the pretty dark-haired baby girl.

Sloane made a mock coughing and choking sound. Niara playfully swatted her arm.

"Get the girl a drink!" Niara called out to Keenan. He gave her a chin lift and began pouring stuff in a glass.

"Oh, I don't think—" was all I got out before the glass was placed in my hand.

"Drink up, bitch!" Niara called out over the two chairs between us. "These two can't drink, so it's just you and me, girl."

When I took a sip, I started choking. "Oh my God, what is that?"

"It's our secret recipe. We call it the magic elixir," she replied in a dramatic, spooky tone. It was strong as hell, is what it was.

Sipping it, I intended to drink the one—and nurse it. But hell if they didn't go down smooth after the first one.

"So, what's Ares's real name," I asked Niara when Sloane and Sage went inside to change the babies' diapers.

"God, he's sexy, isn't he?" she gushed as she grabbed my arm and squealed. I couldn't help but laugh. "Memphis."

"Huh?" I tipped my head to the side.

"His name is Memphis. I heard Raptor call him that once."

Memphis.

I like it.

By the time Sage and Sloane announced they needed to get home with their little ones, I was more than tipsy, I was well on my way to shit-faced. Niara and I were dancing in the firelight.

"I think you need to learn to keep up," Niara practically slurred and I stumbled. Then we both laughed.

"I think it's time for you to get on home," Blade chuckled as he helped balance me. I pouted and gave him my sternest glare.

"It won't work. Let's go, drunkass." He put my arm around his shoulders, wrapped an arm around my waist and walked me back to the cabin. I thought I heard Niara mutter "lucky bitch" as I walked off.

Blade helped me inside and over to the bed where I practically fell face first amid hysterical giggles. It was so comfy, I just stayed there with a dopey smile on my face.

"Sweet dreams, pretty girl," he whispered before he let himself out.

I'm not sure how long I laid there before I couldn't stand it anymore. I needed to pee and all I could smell was the smoke from the fire. With a wrinkle of my nose, I rolled to my back.

"Whoa." The room spun a little. "Shoulda stopped at one."

Never able to handle the smell of smoke on me if I wasn't at a bonfire and outside, I had to get up and get cleaned up.

After rolling my ass out of the too comfortable bed, I shuffled to the bathroom to shower.

The cabin Ares called home was surprisingly cute and bright, but the bathroom was on the small side. If I closed the door, the mirror was too fogged up to use when I was done. With him being gone, it was no big deal.

A sigh passed my lips as I cupped my breast in one hand and dipped between my legs with the other. If I closed my eyes, I could imagine it wasn't my touch on my skin—the heated water like a caress as I rocked back and forth under its spray. Maybe I was drunk and that was my excuse, but fucking hell, I was horny.

As my movements became frantic and the heel of my hand circled over my clit while my fingers curled in that perfect way, I moaned. In my mind, I heard him utter my name in that sexy octave that was nothing but pure lust. My fingertips plucked and twisted at my nipple as I imagined he would.

In the moment that it all became too much, and the

ache grew exponentially until it was an explosion, I cried out his real name—the one Niara told me was his real one.

"Memphis."

Slumped against the wall of the shower, I prolonged the pulses of pure ecstasy as long as I could before my hand stilled. I let out a shaking breath. "Whoa."

One might call it Stockholm Syndrome, but I wasn't truly his captive. There were no locks on the doors. I was free to go up to the clubhouse, I moved freely around the property from here to there. My only restrictions were not to go by the front fence line or to the back of the property. No worries there, because—snakes? No thank you.

The absolutely wild part of all of this was, there was no denying I was more than a little obsessed with the man that had kidnapped me from my brother's—ugh, no—George's home. The massive seven thousand plus square foot house that I was told was impenetrable.

Lies.

The man slipped into that house as easily and slyly as he snuck into my head. It wasn't fair that he affected my body in ways that should be sinful without so much as laying a finger on me.

In the time I'd been his "captive," I'd catalogued all the things I practically melted over.

Of all of them, his smile—reluctant and rare—was my favorite. Then there was that body that fit the name he went by—Ares, the god of war. Everything else was just as potent though. The way his sandy blonde hair always started slicked back but eventually fell free and obscured his crystal blue eyes. The way he looked when he crashed on the couch after whatever he did all day. The way his thick dark lashes fanned his cheeks when he dozed off shortly after dropping to the cushions. The way my fingers trailed over the firm muscles that rounded his shoulders when I covered him with the blanket. All of it made me want things I shouldn't.

Made me *crave* them.

Yet he wouldn't touch me.

It might make me crazy, but I needed one taste. One tiny sampling to take with me when I left—if I ever left—but that was somewhere I wasn't ready to go yet.

Which was why, when I got out of the shower and heard him moving around in the living room, I didn't shut the door. Because I had a direct view of him in the mirror, I knew he could see me too. It might be insanity, and maybe a bit of the lingering liquor, but I was going to seduce him if it killed me.

The fragrant lotion that had arrived when he'd grabbed my bags, was like whipped cream. It left my skin silky soft and smelling downright edible. There was no way he couldn't smell it out there.

With my back to the room, I dropped my towel. I didn't imagine the hissed breath. Nor did I imagine the soft groan when the silky tank slithered down my upstretched arms to settle on the top of the matching thong. A pair of cutoff shorts so short they should be illegal completed the outfit. Maybe the girls were a little too big to go without a bra, but I didn't care.

"Oh!" I feigned surprise when I turned with my towel in hand. I could feel the cool air of the room telling me that my hair had left a wet spot over one side of my chest. His gaze was fixated on my peaked nipple before I saw his throat bob and he leaned forward to grab his phone.

"Hey," he mumbled as he stared at his phone. "Little cold out there for that."

Was that a pink tinge on his scruff-dusted cheeks? *Oh Memphis, I have you now and you don't even know it.*

"Well, I wasn't planning on going back to the clubhouse tonight, so I figured I'd be comfortable in here," I smoothly replied as I sat at the other end of the couch and propped one foot on the edge of the coffee table. Then I absently dragged my other foot up and down my other calf.

He gave a noncommittal grunt and I had to hide my smile as I towel-dried my hair.

The silence grew until it hit an uncomfortable point. "So, what's your end-game?"

"Huh?"

"Your end-game. You didn't kill me, which I appreciate. To my knowledge you still didn't ask for a ransom. Yet I'm still here until after you deal with George," I explained. Not that I wanted them to ransom me, because I didn't want my dad to know what had happened. Thankfully, he'd told Rhonda their phones and laptops would be locked up the entire time they were gone because it was their time. If not, he'd have search parties out looking for me when I didn't answer his calls.

"How will I get home?" Though I asked the question, it was the furthest thing from my mind.

Climbing in his lap and grinding over the bulge I could see forming in his jeans was what I was currently thinking about. It was all I could think about.

The air got thick, and I licked my lips before dragging my lower lip through my teeth.

When I looked back up at him, his eyes were dark, and his lips parted.

And I realized I was cupping my breast.

NINE

Ares

"IT WON'T LAST"—BLACKTOP MOJO

Thinking about the way she smoothed lotion over her skin after her shower, I had to adjust myself. The way her hands followed her curves and dips burned into my head so deep, I couldn't ever unsee it. Especially considering she knew I was there and that I could see her in the mirror.

She wasn't supposed to affect me, Goddammit. That's not why she was here.

Yet for the last several days, she was all I could think about.

Obsessively.

Now she sat next to me on the futon couch and her hand had slowly dropped to cup her tit.

"What are you doing, Ember?" I barely recognized my strangled voice.

Her chest rose and fell under her hand. When she wet her lips again, with her eyes locked on mine, she pinched her nipple. I groaned. Then it was like any restraint I had, disintegrated. The fine thread holding it at bay, snapped.

And so did I.

Twisting, I reached across the void between us and grabbed her. Easily manhandling her small frame, I settled her so she straddled my lap. Hands still gripping her soft hips, I thrust up, pushing my now raging hard cock against her. Fuck, it felt good. Even with layers of fabric between us.

I took one hand and tangled it in her hair, wrapping the braid around my hand and tugging. It exposed her neck that I needed to taste like I needed my next breath. I ran my tongue from the divot at the base of her throat, up and along her jaw, then nipped the soft skin under her ear.

She gasped and I used her hair like a handle to bring her parted lips to mine where I pierced my tongue in to find hers. Not a moment's hesitation and she stroked and twisted hers with mine. Like the animal that rested within me, I was wild, but so was she.

I released her hair to slip my hand under her shirt to cup her tit. Her small hands framed my face as she continued the needy and soul shattering kiss.

When we broke for air, both of us gasping, I nipped her tempting flesh—everything in my reach—and tweaked her pert nipple. Against her warm, sweet flesh, I murmured, as I allowed my lips to trail against her.

"You are a little flame, aren't you? Lighting a fire in me I never asked for, but I can't put out."

She moaned and rolled her hips to rub along my length. I drove up against her and she released my face to fumble with the button of my jeans. The second she unzipped them, she slipped her fingers in my waistband and curled them around my hard length. I hissed an inhaled breath and bit her shoulder.

"Commando?" she gasped.

"Yeah, I didn't have any clean underwear," I growled against her.

Chaos ensued and we tugged and tore at each other's clothes. I think I ripped her shirt off. How the fuck her shorts and thong got off, I don't remember.

With my jeans only down to my thighs, I lifted her enough to suck her hard nipple in my mouth. She lifted up and my eager cock bobbed. Cupping her pussy in my hand, I groaned against her tit at how wet she was. Dipping one finger in and out as I pulled away, we both were frantic and desperate as I lined up and dragged her down. My cock speared her dripping wet cunt and we both cried out.

"Fuck, you're so goddamn tight," I moaned as she was working me in deeper and deeper, inch by inch until I was balls deep in her hot pulsing sheath. "So fucking good," I whispered.

"God, yes," she whispered back as she began to ride me.

Things quickly got out of hand, and she was sliding up

and down on my shaft as I greedily sucked and played with her full tits that bounced in front of me. Using my hips like a piston, I thrust up into her perfect pussy.

Warning bells went off in the back of my mind, but too wrapped up in her, I silenced them.

Her nails scored my shoulders and her teeth left marks on my neck and my chest. I returned everything she gave. "My pretty little fairy."

"Yes," she gasped, stiffening in my arms. Seconds later, her pussy violently spasmed and squeezed me until my eyes damn near crossed. "Yes, yes, yes, yes," she chanted.

Mind separate from my body, my hands found her waist and slid up her sweat-slicked back. They were everywhere at once, gripping and grabbing as I drove up into her. Finally, I couldn't stand it anymore and I got up with her still wrapped around me.

Uncoordinated, I worked my pants down and kicked them off, half stumbling in the process.

Sloppy and feral, we kissed as I made my way to the bed. Something furry hissed and scurried out of the way, but I was too far gone to care about the stupid cat.

In our haste, her braid had lost the tie and her golden hair was falling in loose waves around her. Panting, I stared down at her, cataloguing the red marks I'd left on her flawless skin. Marks that told the world she was mine.

Mate.

"Yessss," I hissed and plunged balls deep in her tight sheath. "Fuck you're so wet. You came all over me, didn't you?"

"Yes, oh God yes."

The sloppy wet sounds we made—knowing I'd done that to her—everything was driving me insane. I was insatiable, greedy, desperate.

Primal.

And from the look in her eyes, I wasn't alone.

But when she lifted her legs and wrapped them around my hips, I completely and totally lost my fucking mind. Over and over, I pounded into her, mesmerized by the way her luscious tits bounced each time I did.

Sweat ran down my back and her hands slipped as she clutched and clawed at me.

Both seeking something neither of us could articulate, we stared in each other's eyes as I fucked her in the basest, most carnal joining of my life. Glancing down, I caught sight of my cock sliding in and out, glistening with her pussy juices and I broke.

"Holy shit, I'm gonna come," I half gasped, half groaned.

She tightened around me and through gritted teeth growled, "Yessss. Come in me."

"I'm gonna fill this tight fucking cunt with my cum. Paint you in it. Make you mine." My words were practically snarled, babbled nonsense as my spine tingled and my balls pulled up. Braced on one hand, I slipped the other down to where I thrust harder and harder. The little whimper that left her lips, told me I was doing just fine. I flicked her clit, then pinched it hard as I fucking shattered and she screamed my name.

"Memphis!"

Head thrown back, muscles tense, I roared out my release and saw motherfucking stars. The world as I knew it changed. It blew apart and reassembled, leaving me disjointed and trembling. Dick still buried deep and pulsing, I dropped to my elbows and buried my face in her neck.

Tasted the saltiness of her skin.

Reveled in the way she dug her nails into me as she continued to throb around me.

Died a little inside.

Acknowledged a truth that made no sense.

She. Was. Mine.

We must've dozed, because the first time, I found her in my sleep, my subconscious needing her in a way I wasn't prepared to process yet.

The next time, I woke to find her tracing my tattoos with her tongue. Blonde hair curtaining her until she glanced up, still tasting me. Those baby blue eyes locked on mine, and I stabbed my fingers into the silky, tangled mess to hold her to my chest.

With teasing little flicks, she circled my nipple. I hissed on my inhale and growled as I exhaled. In a swift motion, I rolled her to her back, cupped behind her knee to lift her leg, and teased the head of my shaft against the now dripping pussy I was going to fill again. She was so wet, I drove in hard and was fully seated in one forceful thrust.

Rolling my hips, I teased with shallow dips as I rocked into her slippery core, then impaled her with hard, punishing movements—demanding she give me everything.

This time was slower, yet no less intense. With each touch, I worshipped her body. With each soft little sound I pulled from her, I became more possessive. I grew covetous of those little sounds of pleasure. Never wanting another man to hear them uttered from her kiss-swollen lips.

She groped me as I steadily continued, never letting up until she began to tighten around me with little pulses giving way to her sweet, sweet pussy contracting as I buried myself deep and came like it was the first time instead of the third.

It was in that moment of clarity that I froze. Cum fresh from my dick to her pussy, I realized not once had we used anything.

"Jesus Christ," I muttered as I dropped my forehead to rest on her chest.

"What?" she asked, panting and breathless.

"I didn't use a condom. None of the times."

"I know. I realized that after the second time, but also realized it was too damn late. I have a patch, but I hope you don't have anything because I'll be mad as hell at myself and you."

I couldn't help it, I laughed into her cleavage. "It's been… a long time for me. And I've never gone without a condom which is why I can't believe I did that with you."

"Now what?" she whispered.

"I don't know," I honestly replied.

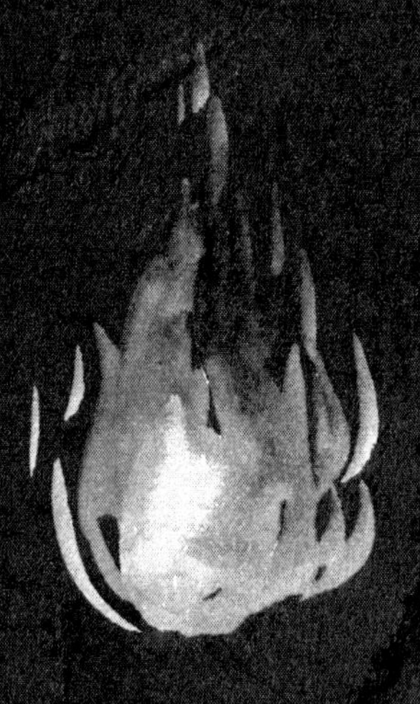

TEN

Ember

"THE DREAM"—IN THIS MOMENT

It had been almost a week since I'd been "kidnapped." With the way things played out, I didn't feel right calling it that. Three days had passed since that hot, wild night in the cabin.

Three days.

Three days and he had barely looked at me since. Things that had developed into a comfortable coexistence had skidded to a stop. When he spoke to me, it was while he was doing something else so he could keep his attention on whatever it was and not me.

He worked sun up to sun down. No clue, what he did, just that he was gone.

And it hurt.

I thought we'd had a moment.

Then I woke up to an empty bed and things had been tense ever since. I debated whether to try again. But I wasn't sure. Rejection was painful.

Tonight was New Year's Eve. My parents would be back in another three weeks. If this week had gone by so quickly, the next three would too. We had limited time to get this figured out. If there was any "this" to figure out at all. I couldn't have read the night so very wrong.

"So, you're telling me it was the best sex of your life," Niara clarified with an arch of her slender red brow.

We were sitting in the clubhouse drinking. The guys had gone out on "a job" so it was just us and Keenan. Who, by the way, was hot as fuck, yet I had no sexual attraction to whatsoever. Not for his lack of flirting, either.

I tipped up my glass, finishing the delicious alcoholic concoction and held out my empty for a refill. Niara poured more of the secret drink from the pitcher into our glasses until it was empty. The women were very close-mouthed about the ingredients.

After taking a drink, I licked my lips and wiped my mouth with the back of my hand. "Damn that's good," I announced.

"You're stalling," Sloane teased in a singsong voice. She raised her glass. "To great sex and girl's nights."

"Here, here," Sage agreed, clinking her rim to Sloane's. When they'd showed up at the cabin door telling me it was pump and dump night, I was confused. Not taking no for an answer, they dragged me with them to the clubhouse. That was about two hours ago—and innumerable drinks with as many different topics discussed.

"Where do you think they are?" I asked as I cast what I knew had to be a longing glance toward the door. Feeling too tipsy to care, I sighed.

"Now back to the best sex," Niara prompted as she propped her chin on the heel of her hand.

"He was… wild. Uninhibited." I glanced over toward Keenan to see if he was paying attention to us. Thankfully, he was busy on his phone. I whispered, "He made me come so many times. I've never come with a guy… you know… in me."

The three of them wore matching expressions with jaws unhinged and eyes wide. Sloane was the first to snap out of it. "Never?"

"No. Not that my experience is vast, but enough that I thought I was broken or something."

"I mean, Phoenix was my first, but I'm on the other side of that fence. I guess he spoiled me because good God can the man work that dick." Sloane giggled.

We all jumped when Keenan sat a new pitcher on the table. "That's disgusting. I never wanna picture that. Ever."

"Do you think they are identical in *every* way?" Niara asked as she leaned back and boldly stared at Keenan's crotch. She went so far as to take her pointer finger and bring it within an inch of the impressive bulge in his jeans.

"Dunno. Not gonna look to check." Sloane shrugged and sipped her drink through her straw.

"Ladies. I'm right here," he cried in exaggerated horror

as he thumbed his chest. Then his mouth kicked up in a sexy smirk as he winked at Niara. "But I'll show you mine and you can pretend you've seen them both."

Sage snorted and I couldn't be certain, but her drink may have come out of her nose. "That was so damn lame," she told him with an eye roll.

Sloane got wide-eyed and glanced from Sage to Keenan, then back to Sage. "Hey! You've seen Phoenix! You could look and tell us!"

It was my turn to be dumbfounded. "Excuse me?"

"Hell, no." Keenan covered his junk. "You think I have a death wish? No way." He walked off grumbling about crazy women thinking he was an idiot and him not showing his dick to the prez's ol' lady. I was still stuck on the fact that Sage had obviously seen Phoenix's package and Sloane was okay with that. What the hell was the story behind that?

A commotion by the door caught my attention and the guys all poured in the door, peeling off warm layers. The fourth one in was Ares. His gaze found me, but quickly averted, and my heart sunk.

"It doesn't really matter because now he doesn't want anything to do with me," I muttered, staring into my glass.

He passed behind me and I knew it was him, because I caught the scent of his cologne. Him being in the same room with me fucked with my body in crazy ways. The awareness that skated over my skin was electric.

When the barstools scraped on the concrete floor, I refused to look over my shoulder. "Where did he go?" I whispered to Niara.

"He's standing at the end of the bar talking to Raptor and Gator," she replied.

My shoulders sagged in both relief and disappointment. "Jesus, was I really that bad?"

"Sweetheart, if he went back for repeats, you didn't suck. I can promise you that," Sage told me with a sly grin.

"Yeah?" Hope bloomed in my chest, and I hated it.

"Oh yeah," Niara confirmed.

"What do I do?" I practically whined.

"You seduce him again," Niara matter of factly replied with a shrug and a sip of her drink.

"How the hell do I do that when he barely even looks at me? And do none of you realize how bizarre this situation is? I've known the man less than a week. We slept together after a few *days*. Not to mention I ended up here under… unusual circumstances. Nothing about us is conventional."

Sloane and Niara shared a look that I didn't understand before Sloane made a slight movement like she was brushing something across the table. Then the drink pitcher slowly slid across the table toward me. Niara made circular motions and the ice cubes began to spin, making a tiny whirlpool.

With my eyes bugging, I dropped my gaze to my cup. "I need to stop drinking," I whispered to myself. Both women chuckled. Niara leaned in and I looked into her mesmerizing eyes.

"We live with the unconventional every day. Most people just have no idea. That's the least of what we would worry about. Things happen when they are supposed to. Whether that's today, tomorrow, or five years from now. Your paths may have crossed dozens of times and you simply never knew," Sloane softly explained.

"Whoa." I dropped my upper body down to look under the table for a rational explanation for what had happened. There was nothing but the wooden bottom of the table under there—and a couple of lumps of chewed gum. Gross.

My head spun when I sat back up too fast, and I gripped the table edge.

"Tell me this," Niara began. I gave her my undivided attention mimicking her early pose of my chin on the heel of my hand. "How do you feel about him?"

I snorted. "Girl, I would let him put it in my butt. Like I would totally do that for him. And you know how I feel about butt-stuff." We'd discussed that earlier too—things we'd done or would do versus things we wouldn't.

Choking ensued behind me and I froze.

"Kill. Me. Now." I mouthed to the table.

My three new friends laughed so hard, Sloane had to run to the bathroom to pee.

ELEVEN

Ares

"THE REAL LIFE"—3 DOORS DOWN

"Girl, I would let him put it in my butt. Like I would totally do that for him. And you know how I feel about butt-stuff."

I choked on my beer, resulting in Phoenix smacking my back repeatedly.

"Dude, if you don't nail that shit down, I'm going for it," Keenan said as he set a new beer in front of his brother.

Reacting from somewhere deep in my dark heart, I lunged up and grabbed him by the neck of his shirt and dragged him toward me until we met halfway over the bar. He was wide-eyed with shock, but I sensed no fear there. "If you ever plan on getting patched in this club, you will never say anything like that again."

"Dude, I didn't know. You didn't say and… you know what? Never mind. I got it." His gaze darted to his brother who had a hand on my arm that still gripped his T-shirt fabric.

"Ares." Phoenix softly called my name, and I drew in a deep breath. For a moment, I held it then let it out with a whoosh.

"Sorry," I muttered to Keenan as my chest heaved with the effort it took to calm myself down. "That was a dick move."

"Hey, man, I'm just a prospect. And I get it, but I truly had no idea she was yours."

Mine.

Was she?

Because the next morning after I'd fucked her so hard and so many times, I'd lost my soul somewhere in her body, I'd left. I'd seen all the marks I'd made on her, and I'd freaked out.

Yet the last few days of avoiding her had me tense, irritable, and fucking miserable.

It was like I was going through withdrawals from the worst drug known to man. My body literally ached for hers. The last few days were a nightmare. Between the rotten way I felt and working non-stop on tracking George down, I was at my breaking point.

"Hey. You deserve someone, too," Phoenix quietly pointed out.

"But do I? You know what I'm capable of." My gaze pleaded with him to tell me I wasn't a fucked-up piece of shit. "What if I hurt her?"

"You won't."

"How do you know?"

"Because when it comes to the ones you love, your cat won't let you hurt them," Raptor said as he sat next to me at the bar and motioned for Keenan to get him a shot. "I've been watching you the last few days. You're miserable when you're denying yourself. Did you know that? The reason I pushed you that first night is because I wondered if there was more to your refusal to kill her—if your reaction was potentially alluding to her being your mate."

My cat's constant reference to "mate," made more sense now. He wasn't referring to just fucking her, he was telling me she was our possible mate. Because I'd spent the last eight or so years trying to repress him, we were… disconnected.

"No one would blame you if you moved on," Phoenix added.

"And the shed?"

"Can wait until tomorrow," Raptor replied.

A quick look over my shoulder showed me long golden waves hanging down her back as she bottomed up her cup. I hadn't been good enough for Tasha. No way was I good enough for Ember, but that didn't mean I couldn't protect her until my dying day.

The stool scraped back as I stood. Then without another word, I took the five steps to her table.

"Ember, can we talk?" I asked her trying to stay quiet. To my relief, she got to her feet. Her tiny frame delicate but tougher than she appeared. The second she lifted those bright blue eyes to mine, I was a goner. It wasn't what I planned on, but I speared my fingers into her hair and leaned down to kiss the lips I'd been dreaming about each night since I finally tasted her.

Our tongues met at the same time as I gripped her ass and lifted. She immediately wrapped her legs around my waist and clung to me. The sweet taste of whatever she'd been drinking only spurred me on. The catcalls and whistles barely registered as I began moving toward the door. I couldn't stop. I kept one eye on the exit as I tangled my tongue with hers again and again.

A little voice in the back of my mind warned that this was a mistake, but I ignored it because I didn't want to hear it. I needed her.

Out in the cold, I strode to the cabin where I struggled briefly with the handle. When it gave way, we practically fell through in our haste. Instead, I slammed the door closed and pushed her up against it.

"This is crazy," she gasped between kisses.

"It will never work," I panted as I moved to her jaw then down to her neck.

"We don't even know each otherrrrrr." She moaned out her last word as I bit the sensitive spot where her neck met her shoulder.

"But fuck I need you," I admitted as I sucked and bit that golden spot.

"Yes. Yes. Yes."

Like the last time, we fumbled with our clothing. I kept her body pressed to the door as I shoved her pants and panties down. My hand palmed her ass, holding her in place. Patience gone, I unfastened mine and pushed them out of the way enough to free my aching cock. We adjusted the tilt of our hips to line my tip to her wet slit. Then I dropped her down until she took every inch I had to offer.

She gasped.

I groaned.

Then I fucked her like I'd been wanting to for three god-damn days.

Cheering and the sound of horns carried through the air from over by the clubhouse as I lay on my back, one arm flung over my head, the other cradling her to my side. One shapely leg was resting over mine and her pillowy-soft tits were pressed to my ribs while her head rested over my heart.

"Happy New Year," I murmured, staring at the ceiling.

She lifted her head and propped her chin on her splayed hand, and I dropped my gaze to hers. Her wheat-gold hair was a tumbled mess, but I'd never seen anything sexier in my life. I brought my hand down to drag my thumb over her swollen lower lip. She caught it in her teeth, then kissed the tip.

"Happy New Year," she whispered.

Inside, I knew that no matter what connection we had, my life was nothing like hers and what we had could never last. Eventually, she'd find out the things my club and I did, and she'd be repulsed by me. But I shoved all those thoughts away with the promise that I'd take things with her one moment at a time until the day came that we had to end.

She wrapped her soft hand around the top of my shoulder and pulled herself up. Her naked body slid along mine and my dick stirred again. Face to face, we were cocooned in the curtain of her hair. Gently, she brushed her lips over mine—not really a kiss, but so fucking breathtaking.

I rolled her to her back and proceeded to kiss and taste every inch of her delectable body.

Later today, I needed to spend some time in the shed.

We'd received a gift from the Cedar Creek chapter by way of my uncle's chapter and the Ankeny chapter. But for now, I was going to get lost in her body as we rang in the new year.

TWELVE

Ares

"TIED MY HANDS"—SEETHER

Come to find out, Wrecker from the newly formed Cedar Creek chapter was a dreamwalker. In his "travels," he inadvertently came across George's location. They had contacted Raptor, who reached out to my uncle's chapter since George was hiding out in an underground sex club he owned in Minneapolis. My uncle, Ox, was one of the members who captured him and brought him down to Ankeny, then they brought him to us by way of Squirrel who had a gift I wasn't about to question because it freaked even me out.

"Who did you sell Ember to?" I asked George Horacio

as I twisted the blade I had pushed into the vulnerable lower side of his chin.

Dragon, Wrecker, and Animal leaned against the back wall. The president, enforcer, and tail gunner had traveled the four hours up from Cedar Creek to offer any assistance we might need.

"You can kill me if you want to, but it's not going to gain you a fucking thing," he ground out from behind clenched teeth. I'd give it to him, the man had balls. He had to know he wasn't making it out of here alive. Yet he was remaining tight-lipped.

"That's where you're wrong," Raptor grimly chimed in from behind me. "I'll gain endless pleasure from your screams as we pull your intestines out through a one-inch hole. That's one of Blade's specialties, you see."

"Fuck off. I'm not telling you shit. I'll be getting the last word and you don't even know it. Because he will come for her—he's like that. As far as he's concerned, she belongs to him. He will mow this joke of a club to the ground," he spat. Yet despite his bravado, a bead of sweat trickled down his brow and dripped off his nose.

"She's not an object to be bought and sold or bartered for. She's your sister, you sick fuck," I snapped.

An almost maniacal laugh erupted from him. "My *sister?* Are you fucking kidding? My mother married her father because she couldn't stand the thought of losing her social status. I didn't ask for a new daddy or a little sister any more than I asked for my dad to dump my mom for his fake-titted assistant."

A gasp followed by a sobbing sound interrupted my focus.

Fuck.

"I fucking see you! Little fucking cunt, this is *your* fault! I hope you're happy!" George screamed and thrashed, causing the chains that fastened him to the ceiling joist to clang.

I turned in time to see Ember spinning on her heels and running.

"Go after her," Raptor murmured. "We've got this."

Before I did, I drew back and nailed George in the face. The satisfying crunch of his cartilage under my fist was followed by blood spurting from his nose.

As I shook out my hand, I took off after Ember. I had the advantage as I knew this land like the back of my hand now. That coupled with the fact that my strides were much bigger than hers, allowed me to catch up to her before she got too far.

"Let! Me! Go!" she shouted when I wrapped an arm around her waist and scooped her up. I winced as her heel caught me in the shin. Then I pulled her closer so she couldn't kick me in the junk. She threw her head back and whacked me in the collarbone so hard I thought she might've broken it at first.

"Stop it!" I demanded as I lowered us to the ground. Once we were down, I sat there, holding her in a bear hug as she struggled. Finally, she ran out of steam, and I held her as her entire frame shook with her sobs.

"Baby, stop," I soothed. "I'm so sorry you saw that."

"Th-th-that's why you told me not to go back there," she stammered through her tears.

"Yeah," I softly replied as I pressed kisses to her hair. Letting her cry it out, I held her, rocking slightly as I did my best to comfort her. I hated that she'd seen that—no matter how much that fucker deserved what he was getting.

Some people would say that what we—and the Ankeny chapter—did was criminal. Legally, I knew I was. However, the people who savagely hurt women and children, getting away with it because of who they were, how much money they had, or ridiculous technicalities, was a worse crime. The victims deserved justice and we doled it out.

I was happily a criminal for that.

But not everyone was cut out to witness and process what we did.

As her sobs tapered off and became shuddered breaths, I loosened my hold and turned her to face me. The tracks from her tears and the red splotches her crying had left behind gutted me worse than Blade could do.

"I never wanted you to be a part of that," I explained as I framed her face with my hands and searched her bright blue eyes. She blinked away the last of her tears and wrapped her hands around my forearms. Little puffs of steam billowed up as her heated breath hit the cold air.

"You kill people?" she asked with her brow creased in disbelief.

"It's not that simple," I started, but then stopped because how did I explain the morally gray world I now lived in? Not to mention the variety of gifts and abilities that existed with certain members of the club?

"Why did you go back there when we told you not to?"

"I thought it was because of snakes or wild animals, but I saw you guys heading back there and figured if you were going, I'd be safe with you. I just wanted to get out, but I didn't realize y'all were moving so fast, so I fell behind. Right before I was going to turn around and head back, I thought I heard screaming and that maybe one of you got hurt."

"Shit." I sighed.

"I'm sorry," she whispered.

"Let me take you back to the cabin," I murmured with a heavy ache in my chest. When she didn't reply, I carefully got to my feet, not once setting her down. During the silent walk back to the cabin, she kept her cold nose buried in my neck and her arms locked around my shoulders. I cradled her protectively until we were surrounded by the warm interior of my cabin.

As if sensing the emotional turmoil that had entered the cabin, the fluffy cat that had delighted in being a thorn in my side, jumped from the bed and scurried underneath. Then I sat on the edge of the mattress. When I brushed her tangled hair back from her face, I saw the dried blood on my knuckles and chills skated over my skin.

My heart froze and it took a moment for it to rapidly resume and try to catch up. This was one more reason that I was no good for her. She was a princess.

And she didn't belong with the villain.

"I'll be right back." She nodded, but didn't reply, nor did she make eye contact. Once in the bathroom, I scrubbed my hands clean, then wet a washcloth with cool water. With a heavy sigh, I wrung it out and returned to the bed. Staring into space, she hadn't moved an inch.

I settled on the edge of the bed and gently wiped her forehead and patted her eyes with the cloth. Then I stripped down to my boxer briefs and crawled behind her. Once I had the covers over us, I made her the little spoon to my big.

We didn't talk about it again, but that night I worshipped her as I made love to her. That was the only description I had for what we did. Because I tried to show her with actions, the words I couldn't get out.

In the span of a week, I had fallen hopelessly in love with a woman I couldn't keep.

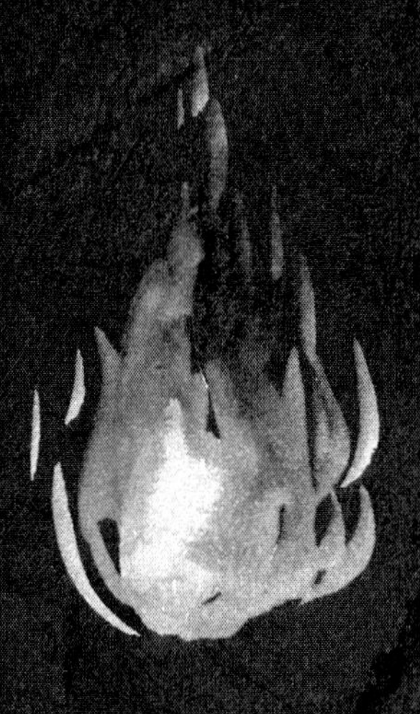

THIRTEEN

Ember

"STAND UP"—SHALLOW SIDE

After the slow, worshipful coupling, Ares—Memphis—had tucked my back into his front and as I stared into space, he drifted off to sleep. I wanted to roll over and wrap my arms around him and never let go. I wanted him to forever be my anchor and my protector.

Because he had misunderstood my reaction.

Had the initial sight of George hanging from the ceiling like a side of beef been a shock? Yes, it absolutely had. But his words were what ripped me apart. The hatred in the vitriol he spewed was beyond ugly and soul shattering.

I'd been a naive fool and that hurt. My life before this suddenly seemed shallow and oblivious. George was a sick, twisted, and selfish person. All things he'd hidden from me for years while I lived my best life. When I thought about how close I'd been to become a statistic—trafficked and blackmailed or one of the missing women of the world that no one hears from again—I wanted to vomit.

What had been revealed over the past week was the stuff of movies, and stories told to children to scare them into behaving.

"I think I love you, but I don't know where we go from here," I whispered to the man who held me, but slept through my confession. Though I was confused, and my thoughts were nothing but chaos, there was still one thing I knew.

We would find a way to be together.

We had to, because crazy as it might be, I couldn't see myself living without him now.

When I woke up alone, I started to panic. My hand slapped to his side of the bed to find it cold.

Then I heard the water running in the bathroom and the sounds of Memphis brushing his teeth. I let the breath I'd been holding, rush out.

Mushu meowed from the foot of the bed.

"Hello, baby boy. Have you started to behave yourself?" I crooned as I reached down to scratch under his chin. He gave me his little chirp of a purr and I smiled.

"No fucking way," I heard muttered from the bathroom.

"You didn't," I whispered as I glared at Mr. Mu who jumped from the bed and went under the futon.

The bathroom door flew open and banged off the wall. "Where is he?" Memphis seemed to grumble to himself.

"What did he do?" I asked with a wince.

"What did he do?" Memphis gave me a wide-eyed, slightly unhinged stare as he repeated my question in a higher-than-normal octave and looked at me like I was crazy.

Then he whipped the towel from his waist to reveal his dick hanging out of a hole in the crotch of his underwear. I couldn't help but stare, because despite its current predicament, it was a beautiful dick. When it bobbed slightly, my lips parted, and I wet them.

"Stop looking at me like that. You're ruining the perfectly justified anger I have for that feline at the moment." When he propped his hands on his hips, the picture he made was too much.

I busted out laughing.

"Oh, you think it's funny, do you?" Dick swinging from the jagged hole in the black fabric, he approached the bed. I laughed harder and he climbed over me until I fell back holding my stomach.

Through it all, I had forgotten I was naked.

He didn't.

Because he held my arms pressed to the mattress and dipped his head to capture my nipple. I sucked in a surprised breath and arched my back. "Memphis," I pleadingly whispered.

"I fucking love it when you say my name," he said between leaving one breast, then latching onto my other nipple.

My eyes rolled and moisture pooled between my thighs at the almost painful way he suckled me. He trailed kisses along my torso, his short beard scraping along the surface until I thought I'd go insane.

Then he began poking at me with his hard on, the spongy tip squishing against me everywhere he made contact. By the end of it, we were laughing like kids, and he was motor-boating my boobs.

"Stop it!" I giggled breathlessly.

"No way. Fuck, I love your tits," he said before he sucked each nipple again, releasing them with a pop.

"Sloane and her mom are having a post New Year's gathering at their shop to celebrate their opening anniversary," I began and he lifted his head to look at me warily. "Could we go? Phoenix, Keenan, and Gator will be there. If you're with me, too, then it should be a safe place. Right?"

"Ember...."

"Please?" I stuck out my bottom lip and fluttered my lashes.

He groaned. "Dammit, don't do that. I'll talk to Raptor. But if he says no, that's final."

"Okay!" I grinned up at him. "We need to get dressed, then, so you can go ask. It starts soon and they could use help setting up."

Turned out, everyone wanted to go. Sloane's mom had ordered custom cookies from a small business to celebrate, and I wanted some of those. I also wanted to get out of the compound for the day. I was bored and ready to climb the walls.

Raptor said I was allowed to go, but I had to try to stay under the radar. So, I plaited my hair in two braids and borrowed one of Memphis's beanies. Then I dug through his drawers and was over the moon to discover what must've been one of Memphis's old high school hoodies. It was worn and soft with what I guessed was a cougar mascot. It was hard to tell, it was so cracked and worn.

"We're taking the SUV so you have less exposure. Besides you don't have the right clothes for the bike," Memphis mumbled as he was typing on his phone. When he glanced up at me after he finished, a crooked grin kicked up the corner of his mouth. "Nice hoodie."

"You like?" I spun with flare, and he chuckled. "Was it yours?"

"Yeah. I actually forgot I had it. Was it even clean?" His nose wrinkled.

I gave the sleeve the sniff-test like I'd done when I found it. "Smells like it."

He shook his head as he rolled his eyes. "You ready?"

"Yep!" I had my hands locked behind me as I spun back and forth.

We piled in the SUV with Keenan and Gator. Raptor was in his truck with Sage, Sam, Seth, and the baby. We followed them, while One Short took the lead on his bike.

"Isn't he cold?" I asked.

Memphis snorted. "This isn't cold."

"No shit," Keenan agreed.

"That's cuz y'all are fucking nuts," Gator grumbled.

"I don't know why you're saying that, because you usually ride come rain or shine," Memphis teased.

I rolled his name around in my mind again. Was it weird that I liked thinking of him as Memphis, now that I knew it was his real name?

It didn't take long for us to arrive. We parked in the alley behind the shop and went in the back door. When we were chilling in the break room waiting for everything to start, a woman that looked too much like Sloane, not to be her mother approached.

"You must be Ember," she observed with a kind smile.

"Yes," I confirmed.

"I'm Annette. The girls have spoken very highly of you," she offered as she held out a hand. When I shook it, she closed the other over mine and cocked her head in question and seemed to study me. "I'm supposed to tell you that she loves you."

A jolt of surprise made me jump. "What?"

She laughed nervously. "I'm sorry about that. Sometimes I get random messages that don't make sense. I shouldn't have blurted that out."

Shaken, I withdrew my hand and shoved it in my hoodie pocket.

"Has your mother passed or a mother figure?"

"Y-y-yes."

"That makes sense then."

At first, I chalked it up to bullshit, because anyone with Google could look up my family. Except somehow, I had a feeling she didn't know who I really was. Chills rippled over me in waves.

As I helped them with the final setup before they opened the doors, I asked Niara if I could borrow her phone to look something up. Guilt hit me that I was kind of fibbing to her.

"Sure, hon. It's in the back room on the table by my purse."

"Thanks." I gave her what I hoped was an easy smile and after making sure everyone was busy with the massive balloon arch they were putting up over the front door, I slipped to the back. After I double checked the date to make sure it was actually the right date and I hadn't lost time without my phone, I dialed my dad's number.

"Hello, Simon Cole, here."

"Hi, Dad. It's Ember."

"Ember? Where are you?" He sounded worried and that was exactly what I didn't want. After Annette had mentioned my mother, I realized my dad and Rhonda would be heading into France today. If he tried to call me and couldn't get through to me, he'd worry.

"I'm with some friends. They are having an anniversary party at their boutique here in Dallas. But I lost my phone somewhere today and I knew you'd be off the ship today. I'm glad I caught you so you wouldn't worry when I didn't answer." I laughed lightly, though I was sick to my stomach, lying to my dad.

"Well, as soon as you're done, go down and get a new phone."

"I will. But honestly, I've kind of enjoyed not having it.

It's crazy how attached we get to them, huh?" I cast a nervous glance toward the doorway. "Maybe I'll see how long I can go without it."

"Sweetheart, I don't think that's a good idea."

I could hear Rhonda in the background asking what was going on. Then dad explained everything to her. "Rhonda said to have George take you down to get one, or ask to use one of his business ones."

My stomach churned at his name.

"No, I don't want to do that. I'm clear across town. I'll be okay."

We chatted briefly about how their cruise had gone, and tears filled my eyes at how much I missed them right now. I blinked them away.

"Okay, Dad, well, they are waiting for me, so I gotta go," I rushed out when I heard voices approaching. "Love you and see you when y'all get home. Enjoy yourselves. You deserve it."

"Hey," Memphis called out. "You okay?"

I had just gotten the phone set down when he came into the break room. As I turned to face him, I carefully pushed the phone under Niara's scarf she had on the table.

"Yeah," I told him brightly. "I just needed a minute. There was a lot going on and my head was hurting."

I was becoming such a liar! Ugh!

He narrowed his gaze suspiciously, and I noted he glanced around where I was. Thankfully, the phone was hidden. Not that I'd done anything wrong, really. It's not as if I called the police. I closed the gap between us and wrapped my arms around his waist.

A soft smile curved his lips. "I don't deserve you," he murmured before he dipped his head and lightly kissed me.

"Why would you say that?"

He didn't reply, but his smile turned a bit sad. Then he murmured, "I think you know."

FOURTEEN

Ares

"M.I.N.E. (END THIS WAY)"—FIVE FINGER DEATH PUNCH

All in all, the day seemed to be a success for Annette, Sloane, and Niara. The shop had a constant flow of traffic with one sale after another. I'd be lying if I said I wasn't ready to go. I'd felt on-edge all day. Though it was good for business, there were too many people in and out. It was hard to keep track of everyone. Which was why I tried to stick by Ember's side.

Torque had even stopped by with his son for a bit and Annette had given the young boy a tumbled Tiger's Eye stone to carry in his pocket.

"Thank you all for your help today," Annette told

everyone as she was pulling the keys to the door from the register. "This was a great day, and I don't just mean the money."

"I'm going to take Sage and Shae home," Raptor said as he approached us. "Do you need Sam and Seth to help with anything?"

"No, Raptor, but thank you," Sloane's mom replied. Sloane was on the phone with her sitter, letting her know we wouldn't be much longer.

"Anytime, Annette," Raptor assured her.

"I'll follow you back," One Short offered, and Raptor nodded. Everyone said their goodbyes and went out the front door, since they had parked on the street. Sloane drew the window curtains that ran behind the displays.

Annette had just locked the door and went to close the blinds on the door when a guy rushed up and knocked on the glass.

"I'm sorry, we're closed," Annette apologetically told him.

"I know, I'm the one who's sorry. My daughter sat her doll down in there and we didn't realize it until we got halfway home. She's losing her shit and my wife is about to kill me since I was supposed to be watching our daughter while my wife shopped." He gave her a pleading smile and folded his hands together.

Annette chuckled and unlocked the door again. "Of course. Do you know where it might've been?"

Right as she turned her back, he grabbed her, reached behind his back and held a pistol pointed at her temple. "No one move. I *will* shoot her," he warned when we all reached for our weapons.

At those words we stopped in our tracks.

"Weapons on that center display," he motioned with his chin. I glanced toward Gator, and he silently nodded. The second all our guns were on the table, and we'd stepped back like the man instructed, the bell over the door rang.

"Well, what do we have here? You didn't need to hold a party on my account, but I will take my gift," the man in the center said with a heavily accented voice. I couldn't quite place it, but I was leaning toward Russian. Ember stiffened next to me.

"What gift is that?" Gator asked, taking charge.

"The pretty little flame," he murmured as his gaze locked on Ember. Suddenly, the pieces fell into place. "I believe she belongs to me."

Belatedly, I recognized the man as Albert Tarasov. Albert had taken over after Sergei Miloslavsky had been killed. If I remembered correctly, Raptor had said something about Sergei going after Hawk's daughter.

The only thing I would say, is that while Albert was a little sociopathic, from what I'd heard, he was not as bad as Sergei had been. Maybe there was hope that we could find a way out of this.

"Well, you see, then we have a problem," Gator drawled. "Because little Ember there belongs to Ares. That's his ol' lady."

It was a lie, but I kept my mouth shut. Maybe because a part of me loved the sound of it. My mountain lion was rumbling and ready to pounce. It was taking everything I had to hold him back. My muscles trembled with suppressed adrenaline.

"Ahh, that *is* a problem. I don't like problems," he replied. "Problems, how you say? Piss me the fuck off."

"What if we could offer you a deal?" Gator asked.

"Deal? You wish to make a deal with Albert Tarasov?" He laughed, but no one else did.

"What if we could get George Horacio for you instead?" Gator asked with a lift of his chin.

Albert's face went flat, but a flash of anger flickered there momentarily. "You know where George is hiding?" He was deadly calm.

"Yes, we do, but the only way you're getting him is if you agree to back off of Ember." Gator played the game well, and I could see why Raptor wanted him as his VP.

"And if I agree to this, how do I know you actually know where he is? And that he's still there?" Albert asked.

"Because we have him," Gator matter of factly replied with a shrug. "We can have him delivered to you tonight."

Albert stared Gator down, then suddenly burst out laughing. "You think I will fall for that? I think not. You take me to him."

Gator and Phoenix exchanged glances, before he said, "I need to call my president before I can promise that."

"By all means." Albert motioned with his hand before he crossed them over his portly belly. "I will wait."

Motherfucker.

Gator stayed in the main part of the store, but stepped to the back corner. He spoke in hushed tones as the rest of us warily waited. Ember subtly scooted closer to me and laced her fingers with mine.

"Raptor said we'll give you George Horacio, but he has conditions that he thinks you'll appreciate," Gator announced as he rejoined us.

"Conditions?" Albert asked with a narrowed gaze.

I couldn't be the only one holding my breath.

"We will meet at a neutral location of your choice within a fifty-mile radius and the delivery happens tonight at nine p.m. and no later. He will also arrange documents that will pass any legal inspection, granting you access and ownership to all of Horacio's solely owned businesses. In exchange for that, there are no hard feelings with our club." Gator crossed his arms.

"And if I refuse?" Albert smirked.

"You'd be a fool to decline this agreement. You make out like a bandit," Gator countered.

Albert's shrewd stare fell on Ember. "I think you underestimate the value that she has to me."

My heart was slamming against my rib cage as if it was trying to break free. Ember's fingers tightened on mine, her breath coming in short, shallow spurts. Inside, fury burned because I fucking knew it was a mistake to bring her here.

"I think… hmm, I think I want one more thing," Albert calmly countered, and dread pooled in my guts. Annette was still held by one of Albert's men, but she was calm and watchful.

"What's that?" Gator asked, but I didn't miss the wary hesitation in his eyes before he spoke.

"Your club owes me one favor that I can collect when I wish," he replied with a dark grin and a casual shrug.

"Yeah, no. We're not making an 'open-ended favor' agreement." Gator scoffed.

"At this moment it doesn't look like you're in a very good bargaining position," Albert countered with a smirk.

"I can't make that call. It's something we would have to discuss with our president. Then we would put it to a vote." I'd never been more thankful for Gator and his diplomatic ways, in my life. Because I would've told this guy to fuck off—Russian mob be damned.

"A vote? Is your president so weak, he must accept what you *vote* on?" When he said that, my cat stirred, and I could feel that slight ripple beneath the surface of my skin.

"No. Our vote makes us stronger because we know that everyone will be behind us in a situation if things go bad. It means we have loyalty and respect. It means we have solidarity. Unity." Gator gave Albert a glower that would've made lesser men quake in their boots. In not so many words, Gator had just told a Russian crime syndicate that we weren't like them—a dictatorship where if we spoke against our president, we would be killed.

Albert laughed. It was a strange, but robust sound that had each of us glancing at the other. From the little I knew about Albert Tarasov, he was a little off his rocker. Rumors abounded regarding his ruthless handling of those who betrayed him or his trust. Yet there was very little documented or verified truth to it, to date. He had entered into a tentative truce with Gabriel De Luca for the Chicago area that Grishka Kalashnik used to control. The details of that truce were kept tightly under wraps, however.

The Tarasovs were distant cousins of the Miloslavskys out of New York. Ivan Miloslavsky had done business with the Kalashniks, and had been heavy into the human trafficking trade. The world I lived in was waiting to see where Albert Tarasov sat as he kept the majority of his business in house and very under the radar. If he had made a deal with George that made Ember his property, that led me to believe he would be continuing the "family business."

Regardless, over my dead body would he get his hands on Ember.

"I like you, Mr. Alligator." He wagged a thick finger at Gator.

Again, we cast uncertain glances at each other. I'm sure I wasn't the only one wondering how he knew so much about us.

"I expect your president to be present for this exchange," Albert finally announced before he snapped his fingers at his men and pointed at Ember. The second they moved toward her we all jumped into action. But we hadn't come prepared for something like this—and we had women present. Albert's men all pulled their weapons, and I thanked the powers that be for Raptor taking Shae and the boys out when he did.

"Whoa, whoa, whoa! Exchange? What are you talking about? No. We're meeting you and you have our word on that," Gator argued.

Again, Albert laughed. "Do you take me for a fool? I haven't lived as long as I have by being stupid. I'm agreeing to this 'trade' as you call it, but I require a deposit of good faith.

Which means, the lovely flame will stay with me until we meet tonight."

A growl rumbled deep in my chest and my vision went hazy. I could feel the crackling in my bones that signified my body was beginning to shift. A hand gripped my arm, and I hissed as I whipped my attention toward that contact.

"Rein it in," Phoenix quietly demanded.

"Then our prospect goes with her," I vaguely heard Gator insist. Keenan stepped forward with his hands held out to ensure he wasn't perceived as a threat.

"Memphis?" Ember whispered in a broken plea. It was taking everything I had to control my inner cat, though and I couldn't answer her.

"He'll be okay, just let me go with you," Keenan softly murmured to her.

The inner war I waged with myself was tearing me apart. On one hand, I wanted to be able to reassure her—be the one who was there for her. On the other, I was fighting to shift and shred anyone that was a threat.

"Ahh, a two for one special!" Albert jovially announced as he clapped his hands together. "Very well. Until tonight gentlemen. I will call you with the location."

"Memphis!" Ember cried as two men guided her away while she tried to tug free.

Phoenix and Gator held my arms as I struggled to go after her. Keenan shot me a glance that said, "I'll protect her" and I had to believe him because I couldn't do a fucking thing without giving away the secrets our club held.

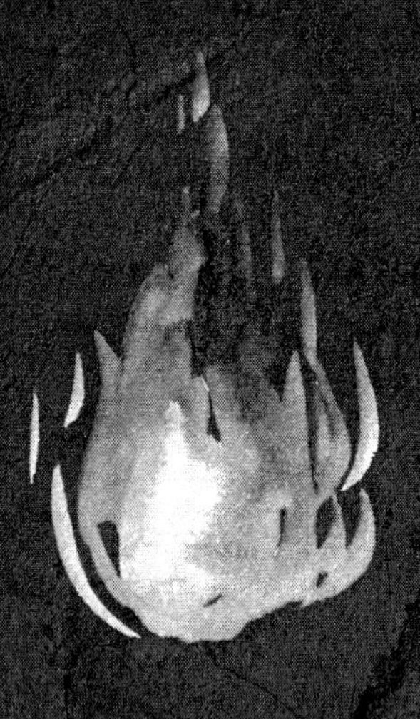

FIFTEEN

Ember

"IRRESISTIBLE"—FALL OUT BOY

My life had become one bizarre turn of events after another. When I thought I was with someone safe, they were my greatest enemy. Those that I thought would be the end of me, turned out to be my saviors. Morally gray? Maybe.

"Are you really going to let me go?" I boldly asked the man sitting next to me. Keenan was in the vehicle behind us, and that made me nervous. Yet, I refused to show that.

He turned to face me.

"You want honest answer?"

I swallowed thickly. "Yes."

"They said you are his woman. Do you love him?" He

didn't need to say who, because I knew exactly who he was talking about, and it wasn't my "brother."

"I barely know him," I hedged.

"That's not what I asked. And time is insignificant when you meet *the one*," he came back with. "I asked if you have true feelings for him."

Staring at my joined hands in my lap, I considered my answer. Finally, I glanced out the window at the passing buildings as we headed further into downtown. Then, I looked back at him. "Wouldn't it be considered a case of Stockholm Syndrome if I was?"

"You didn't appear to be a captive. Is he abusive? Has he been cruel?"

"No! Absolutely, not. If you can believe it, he's been nothing but kind."

"Then I would say just because he brought you to their property against your will, you really aren't in danger. I would call it more of a forced proximity? Or maybe it was fate. Who knows?" He shrugged. "So the answer is yes?"

"I really like him. Love? I'm not sure."

"Mmm. Good enough. Then my answer is yes, if they follow through with their end of the deal, I will let you go." He reached out, grasped a section of my hair, and twirled it around his finger. "Though, I truly don't want to."

When my hands trembled, I curled them and dug my nails into my palms.

The driver of the SUV slowed and pulled into a private underground parking garage. Once he was in a reserved spot, he shut the vehicle off and opened my door. Albert motioned for me to go out ahead of him. The driver held out a hand to help me down, Albert slid out behind me. They weren't giving me any chance to run off.

"Shall we?" He held out his arm for me to take his elbow. Afraid to push him too far, I did as he wanted. The driver took the lead as we made our way toward an elevator. Out of the corner of my eye, I saw the men from the other SUV shove Keenan to get him moving.

We all piled on the elevator and I shot Keenan a worried glance. One of the men used a key card to choose the top floor. Once we arrived and the doors silently slid open, everyone piled out.

Several of the men went out onto the massive balcony and seemed to be checking the area. Like anyone could get up there. It made me cringe that someone would have to be that paranoid. I thought my dad had been bad as I was growing up, but he had nothing on them. It was cold enough, I could see their every exhale.

Albert said something to the men in Russian.

Two of them pushed Keenan back into a chair and he grumbled as he glared at them. Then they tied him down. I could see his jaw ticking from across the room.

Albert went into the bright kitchen and opened a cupboard. "Red or white?"

"Excuse me?" I pulled my attention from Keenan to Albert.

"Wine," he clarified.

"Oh," I wrinkled my nose. "I actually only drink Moscato."

"American women," he chuckled. "You need to broaden your horizons, my dear."

"Why are you being so nice if I'm your hostage?"

"Hostage? It has such a *krest'yankiy* connotation." He wrinkled his nose and waved the thought away.

"What's that?"

"*Krest'yankiy*? It's… how you say… rustic, countryman…." He snapped his fingers. "Peasant."

"Oh."

"You are my guest. That one?" He thumbed toward Keenan. "That one is hostage."

Albert had poured me a glass of wine and encouraged me to sit on the expansive leather couch. After I was seated, he handed me my glass. He took a sip of his, then set it on the coffee table. Using a remote, he turned on a digital fireplace.

"Why did you really want me?" I asked, holding my glass, but not drinking.

He leaned back and rested an arm on the back of the couch. For a moment, I didn't think he was going to answer me. Finally, He sighed and stared sightlessly at the fire.

"When I was a young man, I fell in love. Our father's were… associates. She agreed to marry me and our families were pleased. She was… the love of my life. Unfortunately, she was taken from me, much too soon." He glanced my way again. "I've been a lonely man ever since."

He didn't say how she died, but my imagination ran wild. If he had gotten me from my brother, would that have happened to me, too? Could it still? That gave me chills.

What I could tell from his words and actions was that

he'd never let her go and he still loved her deeply. His silence as we sat there, spoke volumes.

"Tell me about your Ares," he encouraged after he pulled himself from his melancholy musings.

"What do you want to know? Remember, I don't know him that well." I was hesitant to tell him anything in case he was looking for things to use against the RBMC.

I was surprised he knew who Ares was, but it seemed he knew a lot. To appease him, I was vague and spoke more of Ares's personality and the things I liked about him.

While Albert's men guarded the penthouse, Keenan quietly kept watch on us from his position. He may have been bound, but he was ever watchful.

"How did you find me tonight?" I asked.

"If you're going to survive in this life, you need to be more careful. Did you really think I wouldn't be monitoring your father's calls?"

My chest squeezed and my stomach was sick. God, I'd been so stupid.

"No, I hadn't considered that," I admitted with a sigh.

"It's a dangerous world that your Ares is a part of. I hope you're prepared."

"If I'm completely honest with you, I'm not his ol' lady and I have no idea if that's what he really wants. But if he does, I'm willing to give it a shot." My father might not be overly thrilled, but the thought of walking away from Ares was devastating. Imagining never seeing him again made my chest feel like someone had plunged a dagger straight into my heart.

"Over the years, I've learned to read people well. If I

hadn't, it's unlikely I would still be alive." He took a sip of his blood red wine as he watched me. "The man wants you."

We chatted amicably after that. I was surprised that a member of the Bratva could be so personable. The few hours I'd spent with Albert had been almost surreal. While I didn't find him attractive, I found that had George actually given me to him, my life likely wouldn't have been a bad one. Well, for as long as he stayed hearty and healthy—and alive.

One of the men came in and they conversed in Russian. Then he called the rest in.

"It appears it's time for me to take you home, my little flame." He handed me a business card with nothing but his name and number on it. "If he doesn't treat you well, or you ever need my assistance, you call me. I will be there for you in a heart beat."

"Thank you," I replied, oddly touched. Not that I would, because the last thing I would ever want was to be indebted to the Russian mafia.

SIXTEEN

Ares

"FOREVER"—PAPA ROACH

We brought all the family members to the clubhouse as a precautionary measure. Then, Raptor called an emergency church before we would head back to the shed. Blade had been working George over, but George still refused to crack. Not that it mattered now. Because now we knew exactly who he'd "sold" Ember to.

I applauded his tenacity, but it wouldn't do him much good, because Albert wasn't interested in George for his information. He wanted payback—much like Raptor had. I only wished I could be there to help, because I was furious.

"When he calls, we tell him the 'favor' needs to be decided

tonight. I'm not going to be at his beck and call and I'm not blindly agreeing to jack shit," Raptor insisted. His jaw clenched and his hand that rested on the table curled into a fist.

"I agree, but I don't like this," Gator muttered as he thrummed his fingers on the wood.

"Me either. The fact that we're on his radar gives me the heebie-jeebies," Torque muttered.

"Yeah, how does he know so much about us?" Phoenix chimed in.

"It makes sense that it has something to do with Horacio's sister being here. You can thank Ares for that," Blade offered in a bored tone. I bristled, but he was right.

"That's the likely explanation, but I'm not sure that's all there is to this," Raptor mused. There may have been more to why Albert Tarasov had made us his business, but it still confirmed that for as long as Ember was with us, she was my weakness and could be used against me. Which meant she would always be in danger.

"Regardless, let's get Tarasov's package ready. I'd like to make the exchange and be done with this," One Short grumbled.

"I need everyone to be alert and focused. Understand?" Raptor called out with a stern frown. We all nodded. "Good, now let's go get Horacio ready for transport."

"Raptor? A word?" I asked as we exited the chapel. He paused and waited expectantly. I explained my thoughts. He grimly nodded.

"We can make that happen, but I want you to think about it first. Let me know what you decide," he told me.

I inhaled a shaky breath, and let it out in a whoosh. "Will do."

While we were preparing to take the UTV back to the shed, Gator received a phone call. After a brief conversation, the call ended.

"Who was that?" Raptor asked. "Was it him?"

"Yeah, it was Tarasov. He said he'll be meeting us here. As a show of good faith, he said."

"You told him the favor needed to be decided tonight?"

"Yes."

Raptor nodded, then ran a hand through his dark hair in frustration.

We were shocked that Albert had decided he wanted to come here to collect George. It wasn't like the property was a hidden, or a secret. We weren't worried about Albert finding out about our location. He obviously knew a fuck ton about us as it was, it was likely he knew where we were based. It was more of a shock that he would come to the place we have the advantage—putting himself in a vulnerable position.

Which made me worried that he had something up his sleeve.

"Well, Gator, you wait here. Bring Tarasov to the shed when he arrives. One Short, you stay in the clubhouse to work the gate."

On edge, we headed out. We weren't there long.

"Incoming," One Short announced over the radio.

Phoenix, Raptor, Blade, Torque, and I were waiting in the shed. One Short was in the barricaded clubhouse, watching the cameras, and in general, holding down the fort for the family members inside. Gator would wait outside to operate the gate and to guide them back here using one of our utility quads.

I stood out in the bitter-cold night with Raptor, waiting. We could hear the vehicles before we saw the bouncing flicker of headlights once they broke through the cedars. The ATV pulled up next to the shed. The other vehicles stopped several feet away. The dust drifted over the beam of the lights before it slowly settled. No one got out and my entire body was on alert.

"If you can't hold your shit together, I'm going to have to ask you to excuse yourself," he murmured as he kept an alert eye on the two vehicles sitting there. Gator got off the quad and joined us.

"We could've taken them," Gator quietly observed as he watched and waited too.

"Maybe, but there's no way he brought every single one of his men with him, now is there? All it would've taken was one call, and what could that have done to us? It was too risky. Quite frankly, I got my pound of flesh out of George. And this way, we don't have to dispose of the body," Raptor explained with a shrug.

"True," Gator replied.

As we continued to wait, I silently simmered.

"Are you sure you want to do what we discussed?" Raptor asked me.

Swallowing the lump in my throat, I nodded.

He sighed.

"Ares, if you're sure, I think you need to have Dragon see her."

I remained silent. No matter that I knew it was what I needed to do, I couldn't make myself commit—if we brought Dragon in, that made it final. My stomach knotted at the thought.

The first door opened, and my spine stiffened. I practically trembled with the adrenalin racing through my veins.

The first one out, I ignored. The second, was the small framed, delicate pixie of a woman I was waiting for. Albert followed next. Keenan was brought from the second vehicle. They approached us at a leisurely pace, but with each inch that they grew closer, my heart raced faster.

"We meet again, my friends," Albert announced.

Raptor grunted.

We were not friends.

"Keenan, take her back to the clubhouse," Raptor instructed.

"Not so fast," Albert called out. "My merchandise?"

Raptor motioned over his shoulder and Albert followed, but he paused by the door and pointed at Ember. "She waits out here."

A look of understanding crossed between Raptor and Albert before Albert nodded to his man that held her arm.

My gaze darted over her head to toe, ensuring she was truly okay and in one piece. Our eyes met and held. I wanted to touch her, hold her, make sure she was okay. But this wasn't the time.

Reluctantly, I left her outside with Keenan and followed everyone in.

"Ugh! What is this? You have already dirtied him. And he looks dead to me," Albert complained with a wrinkle of distaste in his nose.

Blade grabbed a bucket full of ice water and tossed it in George's face. George gasped and struggled to stand upright. If I had to guess, his shoulders might be dislocated. One eye was swollen shut and the other was nearly as bad.

"Albert?" George choked out in a broken voice.

For the first time, I saw actual bone-chilling fear in George's gaze.

And I reveled in it.

It took Albert's men very little time to move George from the shed to the back of one of the SUVs. Duct tape over his mouth muffled his screams.

"Foul business. Now about that favor," Albert began as he turned to face Raptor.

"We agreed that we had the option of refusing if it was out of our realm," Raptor reminded him.

"Do you think I don't know what this chapter and the Ankeny chapter's specialties are?" Albert asked with a smirk. "I have done my research. It doesn't do to take over an operation and not know who does the dirty work around us."

Raptor remained silent—waiting to see where Albert was going with this.

"That being said, I will need you to dispose of the

body when I am done with him." Albert gave us a dark smile.

Raptor palmed his face.

Albert grew serious. "I needed to know if I could trust you. You have proven you are a man of your word, as are your men."

We didn't correct his terminology.

"I think we could have a very lucrative business agreement. If you so choose, that is. Think about it." He held out a hand and we all held our breath as Raptor stared at it. Then they shook and Albert grinned widely.

We walked him to his vehicle and Albert snapped his fingers. The goons he had with him, set Ember free and she ran to me, jumping up in my arms. I held her so tight, I was afraid I might break her.

"He didn't hurt me," she whispered in my ear. Though I was relieved, I knew that might not always be the case.

And this was my final reason.

I couldn't keep putting her in danger.

Before Albert got in the SUV, he stopped next to us. When I set Ember on her feet, she turned to him.

"Do you know why I wanted you?" the big Russian asked her as he fingered a section of her hair. My teeth ground as I forced myself to remain calm and not break his arm.

"No," she whispered.

"Because you reminded me of my Anastasia," he replied with a sad smile. "George thought I wanted you because you looked young. I might not be a good man, but I am not into such perversions. I saw you once at your brother's house and he spoke to another of how much he could demand for you. I tried to get you then. At that time, he refused because he was waiting for you to reach twenty-one so he could use your trust fund as incentive to bump up your price. When he offered you to me as compensation for my money lost, I knew he was desperate."

To say I was stunned, was an understatement.

"The money meant nothing to me—I had hoped you would come to love me once you were mine." Then he lifted his gaze to look me in the eye. "But at the witch's store, I could see her heart had been taken. Do not hurt her."

As he held my attention, he spoke in Russian to the last of his men. Before he climbed back in his vehicle, he called out to Raptor. "I'll be in touch."

Raptor gave a lift of his chin, and they loaded up.

"Is Dragon still around?" he asked Gator, who nodded. I gritted my teeth.

Gator started up the ATV, then escorted them back out.

The tension coiled within me, slowly eased. I tried to gauge Raptor's mental state, but he was stoic and didn't say a word.

"Blade, Torque, Keenan, gather everything up. Phoenix, torch the evidence."

"Take her back to your cabin. I can call Dragon and have him come over."

"It's okay, I won't need him." If I had to give her up, I selfishly couldn't erase her memories of me.

"You sure?"

"Yeah."

The look he gave me was full of sympathy. I didn't deserve it. I'd done this to myself.

Hand in hand and heart shattering, I walked back to my cabin with her.

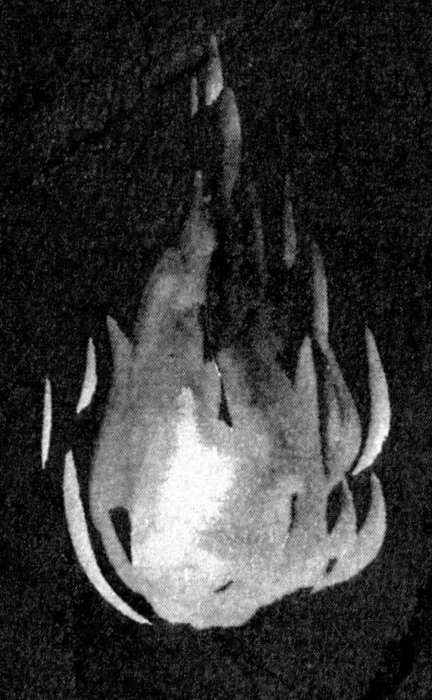

SEVENTEEN

Ember

"DECEMBER"—COLLECTIVE SOUL

Surprisingly, the time with Albert had flown. Then we were leaving again. My nerves were so frazzled by the time we got back to the compound, I thought I'd have a breakdown.

Before he got out of the SUV back at the compound, he had turned to me. "Don't squander what you have. He'll think he needs to protect you, but what he really needs is you by his side."

Then his man had gotten out and helped me down. Albert followed.

My eyes landed on Memphis and the rest was a bit of a

blur. He was all I saw. Anxious, I wanted to run to him, but the tension of the situation held me back.

By the time Albert had driven away with the man I used to think of as my brother, it was late. Raptor drove the ATV back to the clubhouse and I rode in Memphis's lap. With his strong arms wrapped around me, I was safe.

As if nothing had happened and the entire day was a dream, we were back in the cabin. Memphis was quiet as he pulled his shirt over his head. My mouth watered at the ripple of his torso with his movements.

I needed the heat of his body against mine. I needed to touch him, but I also needed his hands on me, making me feel alive—safe.

Featherlight, I traced the tattoos on his chest. He closed his eyes and bit his lip. When I leaned forward and circled his nipple with my tongue, he sucked in a sharp breath. Remaining essentially motionless, he allowed me to have my control as I explored him.

"You're like a work of art," I whispered as I followed the hills and valleys of his sculpted body with my hands and mouth. The way his breathing sped up was one of the only tells that I was affecting him.

That and the way his cock had come to life behind his denim.

Which was why my next move was to unfasten the brass button. I watched him closely as I slowly unzipped him. With his eyes closed he didn't see the way I pressed my lips flat to keep from laughing at the fact that he was commando. My gaze darted around and found Mushu sleeping on one of the barstools.

Little shit.

Ignoring my bratty feline, I went back to my task at hand.

My fingers wrapped around his thick shaft, and I reveled in the silky soft feel of the skin that encased it. Softly, I dragged my lips over the tip, then down each side. I repeated the motion with my teeth. He groaned and I licked the clear bead that appeared before pulling the end into my mouth.

"Goddamn," he whispered as his hands slipped into my hair. Gently, he cradled my head and guided me to show me what he liked. Slowly, I worshipped him and alternated between sucking and licking until he began to thrust a little. Occasionally, I started to gag, but I swallowed, and it wasn't long before he hissed in a sharp breath. "I'm gonna come."

It was a warning for me to take as I would.

His breaths grew ragged, his motions less coordinated, but I didn't stop. When he clutched my hair tightly and drove down my throat, his hot cum splashed the back of my mouth and I swallowed every drop.

"Jesus fucking Christ," he murmured when I let him slip free of my lips. As I wiped my mouth with the back of my hand, he stepped on the bottoms of his jeans and worked them off. He kept his blue eyes on me as I knelt at his feet and stared up at him. Then he reached down, grabbed me under my arms and lifted me.

I squeaked in surprise, but it was cut short when his lips crashed to mine.

The kiss was savage and desperate, broken only when

absolutely necessary, and lasted until he had me naked and spread out on the bed. Then he ventured across my cheek, and sucked my earlobe into his mouth before he nipped it. I tilted my head to grant him access as he moved down my neck and I speared my fingers into his bronzed hair.

I wrapped my leg around him to feel my skin against his.

This was different than any other time. My eyes closed and I lost myself in the slow and sensual meanderings of his talented mouth. The sharp sting of his teeth was soothed with the soft wetness of his lips and tongue. Over my chest he trailed as he licked and sucked each inch before he continued down my stomach to dip into my bellybutton. I shuddered with want and my pussy clenched.

As his hot mouth closed over my aching clit, I whimpered and he slipped one, then two fingers into my throbbing sheath. Slowly, he dragged them over that spot deep inside that drove me higher and higher. My breaths came in pants as I pulled and tugged at his hair. I thrashed and chased that building sensation that I knew would send me into that perfect blissful nirvana.

"Memphis!" I screamed as suddenly, I was there. His talented fingers drew out every last pulse they could until I drifted back to earth breathless with my head spinning.

For a time, he rested his cheek on my lower abdomen, occasionally pressing a soft kiss to the skin. Each time, it tickled and made my stomach tense. Then, when my breathing evened out, he kissed his way back up. He used his tongue to swipe across my lower lip. I opened and he delved in. As our tongues danced, I tasted myself on him and my desperation returned. I clutched at him, unable to hold him tight enough or close enough.

He lifted one of my legs and lined himself up. Thanks to the orgasm he had given me, he slipped in without resistance. I tilted my hips to bring him in as far as I could take him.

"Jesus," he whispered into my mouth, and I whimpered.

Slow but steady, his hips rolled, and his cock filled me over and over. I clung to his shoulders and back. Muscles rolling under his skin, slick with sweat, I fought to hold him and meet each thrust with my own.

Our breathing grew ragged, our motions faster, but we remained wrapped in each other—a tangle of limbs that knew no start or end. Pants and gasps echoed off the walls as we chased the promise of heaven.

The first flutter in my pussy signaled I was nearly there, and I thought he whispered, "yes." A few more strokes and I was there, but so was he.

Together... we shattered.

Later, as I drifted into sleep, cocooned in his arms, it felt like raindrops dripped on my shoulder.

EIGHTEEN

Ares

"A SCAR IS BORN"—THREE DAYS GRACE

When we woke up, I braced myself. As I held her close to my side, I kissed the top of her head.

"I need to take you home today," I told her.

She stiffened in my arms.

"No."

"Babe, your parents will be home tomorrow. Did you forget?"

"Actually, yes," she reluctantly admitted.

"We can't just have your family wondering where you are when they get there."

"I can call them," she offered, the hope in her tone killing me.

"It will go over better if you're there when they get there," I mumbled, unable to meet her gaze.

I was vague when she asked what she should tell them. I was quiet when I helped her pack up what little she had with her. With each second that ticked by, my insides shredded. My cat was restless—angry. He knew what I was getting ready to do and he sure as hell didn't like it.

News flash… neither did I.

It didn't matter that I knew this was how it had to be. I was hollow inside.

Without any specific promises, I got her loaded up in the chapter's SUV with her demon cat in it's carrier in the backseat. She was reluctant, but agreeable—because she thought this was temporary.

"My parents should be home before lunch. Once I've seen them, I'll drive back to your cabin. How did we meet—so we have our story straight?" she asked, breaking the silence. She turned to face me with a bright smile. Except I couldn't reply. My heart seemed lodged in my throat.

"Memphis?" She said my name like a question as she stared at me. The wipers beat a monotonous tune while the rain fell, steady and cold.

As we turned into the driveway, I remained silent. The thought of dropping her off and never seeing her again was shredding me from the inside out. Like my mountain lion was ripping my flesh from my bones as he raged at what I was about to do.

Instead of opening my mouth, I tugged my ball cap lower, kept the brim obscuring my face, and entered the gate code Ember had given me. Once the gate started to move, I rolled up the dark tinted window.

"Memphis!" Her breath was coming in hard gasps when I stopped in front of the house and disbelief furrowed her brow. I avoided the hurt I saw flash through her eyes.

Trying to find my voice, I propped my elbow on the door and pinched the bridge of my nose. I'd gone over this moment all night as sleep eluded me. No matter how prepared I thought I was, nothing could've truly braced me for the tsunami of devastation that was crashing against my defenses. Clenching my jaw, I turned to face her.

"What could we tell them?" I asked in a tone I hoped sounded disdainfully sarcastic. "We met through friends? Because we obviously have friends that run in the same circles. Or maybe the old met at a bar story? Hell, you could tell them that we met at our strip club. That would go over great. Really endear me to the fam, right?"

If it was possible to hear a heart break, it would sound like the stuttering sob that escaped her. Unable to sit there any longer for fear of cracking, I got out, and went to the back door. The rain had already drenched me when I opened it and lifted the crate filled with hissing feline animosity. Once I had Mu in one hand and her bag in the other, I closed the door and carried it all to the covered front porch.

When I saw she hadn't gotten out, I dropped my head. "Fuck."

Even in the pouring rain, I could still see the tears tracking her cheeks as she stared at me. When she pressed a splayed hand against the glass, I inhaled a stuttering breath and tried to breathe through my caving chest.

With determined strides, I stalked to her door and pulled it open. She shrank back and inside I crumbled.

"Ember, you need to go inside."

"No!" she snapped, refusing to get out. I almost wanted to laugh at the picture she made. She reminded me of an angry Tinkerbell.

Forging forward with the plan I knew I had to stick to, I reached over her and unbuckled her. She tried to snatch it back, but I firmly grabbed her hands.

"Stop it. I'm not—" her tirade ended before she could get another word out when I lifted her and tossed her over my shoulder. That had her madder than Mushu. Like a little wildcat, she kicked, arched and fought me with each step I took. Her body twisted and turned, her hands and fists beat on me, but I didn't stop. Instead, I smacked her ass. That immediately stilled her, and I took the steps two at a time then dropped her to her feet.

Unsteady due to being upside down, she wobbled. I held her until she stopped swaying, then let her go like she was on fire.

Unable to be close to her for fear of giving in to my

heart and my mountain lion, I turned tail and rushed away to the vehicle. Except before I could round the front of the SUV, she grabbed my arm. With surprising strength, she tugged, and I turned to face her.

The cold rain poured down, soaking us both to the bone.

"Don't you walk away like that!" Full of fire and fury, she smacked the side of my arm.

"We were never going to work, Ember. Someone like you doesn't belong with someone like me," I painfully explained to her.

"Says who?" she cried and grabbed the front of my shirt. Blonde hair plastered to her head, she shook me. Where once I'd thought she looked like an ethereal fairy, wet and angry, she reminded me of a furious water nymph.

I pressed my lips flat as I shoved my hands in my pockets and looked away. I had to, or I was going to reach for her. Once I had myself under control, I lifted my gaze and stared into her pretty face. Though it was painful, I memorized each nuance for the lonely nights to come. "Says the world."

Though my knees threatened to buckle from the knife that seemed to have been driven into my heart, I stepped back. When she let her hands fall to her sides and she didn't move, my chest collapsed. Breathing was out of the question. Rain ran down her cheeks and I knew it was mixed with the salt of her tears.

Without a backward glance, I ducked my head against

the pelting downpour and walked around the front of the SUV.

"You're a coward, Memphis!" she angrily cried out as I climbed in.

But I didn't reply, and I didn't stop.

Because she was wrong. I was ripping out my own heart to give her a chance at happiness. Something I could never truly give her.

A coward would've kept her—uncaring of what was best for her.

NINETEEN

Ares

"STARS"—SIXX:A.M.

It had been three months since I'd dropped her off in the rain. Each day, I died a little inside. I stalked her on social media. Occasionally, she showed up on a Google search at a function with her parents.

When her "brother" had "died in a fiery crash" her emotionless face had been there from pictures at his funeral. The media loved a tragic death, especially if they were rich or famous. In a few, her stepmom was being consoled by her dad and she stood in the background stoic and cold.

I drank too much.

Keenan and I frequented the little bar down in the

Bishop Arts District down by Sloane's shop. More often than not, I had to leave my bike parked there and Phoenix picked me up and let me sleep it off at the house they were renting next door to Annette's.

"You gotta snap out of it, man," Keenan said from his barstool next to mine. "This isn't healthy."

"Don't care," I replied. I downed the first whiskey of the night and held up my glass to the bartender for another. She gave me a wink of acknowledgement and handed the change to her current customer. Then she poured my drink and swapped my glass out.

A couple of blondes and a tall dark-haired guy sat down next to us. In their own little world, they laughed and joked. For one insane second, I wanted to lean over to see if the blonde that sat with her back to me had hair that smelled like my shampoo.

"I'm losing my fucking mind," I muttered.

"No shit," Keenan agreed.

Then the one that was standing lost her balance and fell into the one sitting who fell back into me. We were like a set of human dominos. My drink that I was bringing to my mouth ended up all over the bar.

"Goddammit," I grumbled.

"Oh my God! I'm so sorry! Here, let me help," the girl next to me said as she grabbed a handful of napkins and pressed them to the golden puddle on the bar top.

Breath stuck in my throat, I froze as I stared into crystal-blue eyes framed with thick dark lashes.

"I'll buy you another. My cousin Giselle is such a clutz."

She flagged down the bartender and ordered me a replacement. The entire time I sat there with my mouth hanging open. She held out her hand. "My name is Ember."

Her cousin Giselle looked over her shoulder, and used her pointer finger to lift my jaw. I swallowed hard and blinked. *I must be dreaming.*

That's when I realized she still held her hand out.

Feeling like a complete moron, I reached out and took her small hand in mine. "Memphis."

"Memphis. I like it. It's different."

"Yeah."

"God, you're a loser," Keenan muttered with a chuckle.

"You don't sound like you're from around here," she observed in a voice that haunted my dreams—the one with the barely there twang.

"I'm originally from Minnesota," I replied, still dazed, but catching on.

The bartender placed my new drink in front of me, but I didn't touch it.

She traced the stitching on one of my patches. "So is this, like a biker vest?"

When she bit her lower lip and looked up at me with a hooded gaze, my dick came to life for the first time in months.

"Y-yeah," I choked out, coughing to clear my throat that my words were stuck in.

"Hmm. You should take me for a ride," she suggested. The sly smile that curved her lips spoke of innuendos that I should've ignored, but couldn't.

"Who's your friend, Ember?" Giselle asked as she lifted what looked like a fruity drink to her lips.

"This is Memphis. He's gonna give me a ride on his bike," she happily announced.

"I am?"

"You are," Giselle confirmed.

"Jesus Christ," Keenan quietly groaned. "I swear to God, you've pickled your brain."

"Well, what are you waiting for?" she asked. It was then that I saw a brief flash of uncertainty in her beautiful blue eyes.

Standing, I pulled out my wallet, and threw some money on the bar. "I'll be back," I told Keenan.

He laughed. "No, you won't. At least not today."

Giselle slid into my vacated seat and flashed a brilliant white smile at Keenan. "This is my brother, Blaine. I'm Giselle. And you are?"

Ember took my hand and I swear to Christ lightning hit me. It kickstarted my heart and I squeezed hers back. She led me outside and stopped by where Keenan and I had backed our bikes up to the curb.

"Which is yours?"

Wrapping my hand around the side of her neck, with the other cupping her denim-clad ass, I walked her backward until she was against the building. Her pulse was frantic against my palm and her lips parted. Hunger heated her gaze.

"What are you doing?" I whispered, uncertain and confused.

"Meeting an insanely hot guy in a bar while I'm out with my cousins," she replied in a breathless whoosh.

"Yeah? And what would Daddy dearest say if I pulled up in front of his house with you on the back of my bike?" I demanded.

"Well, would you believe that when he was young he rode an old Fat Boy?" She held that plush lower lip with her teeth again and I used my thumb to gently pry it loose.

"That's... wild. But baby, you know I'm not good enough for you. There are things you don't know about me," I began, but she lifted a finger and pressed it over my lips.

"I don't care. All I need to know is that I love you and I'm pretty sure you love me, but it would be nice to hear it. At least the amount of money you've blown in there leads one to believe you're trying to drink away a memory. Or two." She thumbed over her shoulder toward the door of the bar.

"How would you know how much I've spent here?"

"You're not the only one with shady connections," she replied as she waggled her brows.

The first real smile in months lifted the corner of my mouth. "Is that right?"

"Yeah. So, about that ride?"

I shook my head as I huffed a short laugh. "You need a helmet."

"Hmmm, like that one?" she pointed at a black helmet with a decal of hot pink lips on the side. It was on Keenan's seat. I cocked a brow at her.

"I wasn't sure which one was yours," she bashfully murmured.

"What if neither were mine?"

"Then I'd have been a little embarrassed." She shrugged. "But I knew it was you guys, because we saw you pulling up, but had to go around the block to find a spot and then I wasn't sure which one was you, but knew one was. Besides, this kind of gave it away," she blurted out in one long breath. Then she pointed at the RBMC decal on my rear fender.

I bent down, grabbed her ass and lifted her. She wrapped her legs around me immediately and I loved it. Then she gave me a quick kiss.

Amazed, I searched her face for any sign that this wasn't real. When all I saw was determination mixed with a little worry, I kissed her back.

"I love you," I admitted, surprised at how terrifying the words were as my heart sped up. It was crazy that we had met the way we did and that we fell hard and fast. Yet everything about it felt so right. Like finding the missing piece to a puzzle.

"Oh, thank God. Now you have a lot of kissing up to do, so let's get started," she gushed.

I full-on laughed. Hugging her tightly, I spun her around.

"Thank fucking God," I heard Keenan say from over by the entrance. The three of them stood there watching us. "He was a miserable fuck to be around."

They all went back inside, leaving us alone.

"I can't believe you don't hate me and that you went to all this trouble to be here and do… all of this." I motioned to the bar and the helmet.

"I'm gonna be honest. For the first few weeks I was pissed. I wanted to find my way back to the compound and beat your ass. Then make love to you, then beat your ass again."

I snorted.

"I kept hoping you'd show up. Or that I'd run into you somewhere. Because I couldn't believe that we weren't meant to be. But then I remembered something Albert had said to me, and I realized how damn stubborn you are."

She glared at me. I had the good sense to appear contrite.

"I knew I had to take this into my own hands. If you had moved on and I was wrong, then I would take my broken heart and navigate my way through my ocean of tears. Except what I found was that you were as miserable as I was. Please don't shut me out again. Open up to me. Let me in and let me love you the way you *deserve*," she pleaded.

A sigh escaped me, because I knew she needed to know everything.

"I have one more thing you have to see before you decide you can handle me. If it isn't something you can deal with, then I'll make it so you don't remember I ever existed. I never want you to be sad because of me. I'd rather you didn't remember me than hate me or be hurt by me." I would be taking a huge chance with this. If I showed her who I really was and she freaked, I would have to have Dragon erase me from her memories. It was what Raptor suggested before I took her home, but I couldn't do it.

"Okay?" She seemed a little concerned and she should be.

Reluctantly, I set her on her feet, then helped her get her helmet fastened properly. I walked her through getting on and what to expect during the ride. Once I was pretty sure she understood, we hit the road. She learned quick and I fucking loved having her ride with me.

After taking the scenic route, I made my way back to the compound. At the gate, I used the sensor we all had to open the gate, and I drove up to my cabin.

"That was amazing!" she squealed as she struggled to get her helmet off. With a chuckle, I helped her, then tried to work some of the tangles out of her hair.

"I should've had you braid it," I apologized.

"It doesn't matter. I'm fine. I'll comb it out later." She waved off my concern and wadded it up in that messy updo thing that made her look sexy as fuck.

Taking her hand, I led her to a more isolated area of the property. I wanted us to be alone for this.

"Have a seat," I told her and motioned to an old stump. Her laughter was like the brightest music and her smile was infectious.

Suddenly nervous as hell, I started peeling off my clothes.

"Oooo, I like where this is going," she drawled with a grin that had me shaking my head at her.

"Later," I promised.

"Holding you to that." She winked.

When I stood before her without a stitch of clothing on, I maintained eye contact and crouched before her. Her smile slipped a bit, and she tilted her head in question. "I'll answer your questions afterward. Okay?"

She nodded. Then, I concentrated on merging myself with my mountain lion and overcoming the pain of the transformation. When I was done, I blinked to clear my vision and saw her smile was gone and her mouth hung open. Face white as a sheet, she stared.

When I took a step toward her, she scrambled off of the stump and held her hands out in front of her. Slowly, she started backing away.

"Wh-wh-what's going on? Memphis!" she called out as if she thought I was hiding somewhere though she'd just watched me shift. Her eyes darted to the sides.

Disheartened, I sat and stared at her. Then I laid down and rested my head on my front paws. I waited to see if she would stay or run. When I didn't do anything, she stood her ground. Inside, I begged her to be brave. I pleaded with her to accept me.

Because if she didn't then it would be as if she died, because she wouldn't know me, and I couldn't go around her.

Please.

She wet her lips and swallowed. Then she lowered her head. When she looked up, there was still fear—which I hated. But there was more. She took a tentative step toward me, and I eagerly lifted my head.

Bad idea, because she backtracked. I quickly put my head back down.

Finally, she narrowed her gaze and stared at me. "Is that really you, Memphis? It's crazy, but those are your eyes," she whispered. With that, she took a step closer.

Then another.

She reached a hand out in front of her. It trembled, but she did it anyway. *That's my brave girl.*

Stretching, she got close enough to touch her fingertips to my fur. "Oh my God. You're so soft."

My eyes closed and I purred at her touch. She jerked back at the sound. I remained still. "Is it okay to touch you? Did I make you mad?"

It sucked that I couldn't talk to her like this. Instead, I pushed my head up into her hand, encouraging her to pet me. Then something utterly amazing happened, she giggled, and she began petting me in earnest. I ate it up.

No one had ever done that—pet me.

She knelt on the ground in front of me and scratched under my chin. My eyes closed in happiness. This could have gone in such a different way.

"No wonder Mr. Mu didn't like you. You were competition," she explained with a small chuckle.

I huffed.

Eventually, she laid on the ground and rested her head up against me.

"I can't believe this. Some women are cougars. I actually *have* one!" I nudged her with my head. "What? It's true!"

After a while, I shifted my position, and she got up. "Did that hurt?"

Putting everything I had into it, I transitioned back. Panting, I stayed there a moment, breathing through the waves of excruciating pain.

"Are you okay?"

"It… hurts…."

"Then don't do it!"

I gave a humorless laugh. "It's not that easy. And it doesn't hurt for too long."

Once I had myself under control and knew my knees wouldn't buckle when I stood, I put my clothes back on. She took my hand and looked at me with compassion.

With a reassuring smile, I led her back to my cabin.

I sat on the couch and tugged her into my lap.

"Do you understand you can't tell anyone?" I asked her, terrified that this was too much for her.

Facing me, she framed my face with her hands. "Memphis, I would never do anything to knowingly put you in danger. I love you."

"Even knowing this is what I am?"

"*Especially* knowing this. Knowing that you trusted me enough to share that part of yourself is an honor."

The corner of my mouth kicked up and I decided not to tell her that if she totally freaked out, I would've had to have Dragon erase her memory. Because all in all, she was right. I did trust her, and I wanted her to accept me for who and what I was.

"I have a question, though." She stroked my cheeks with her thumbs.

"Yeah? What's that?"

"Um, what about children?"

My heart stopped and my gaze dropped to her waist. "What?"

Understanding dawned and she grinned. "No, I'm not. But can you have children?"

"I mean, I'm here." I shrugged. Then I thought a moment. "My mom is a shifter though."

"Was your dad? Wait. What? Your mom is still alive?"

"Yes, she is. We haven't talked in well over a year, but she's very much alive. She'll be happy to hear about you if you think you can handle it." I chuckled, then sobered. "Do you want children?"

She drew in a shuddering breath. "I do, but I'm afraid. My parents had a hard time conceiving. They tried for years, then I finally came along, and my mom died."

"Well, baby, if we're really doing this, then we'll cross that bridge when we come to it. Fair enough?"

She leaned in to press her pillow-soft lips to mine. "Yes."

"And my uncle told me that when a human and a shifter mate, it's kind of a fifty-fifty chance that the child will be a shifter. So, there's that."

"Oh. Wow."

"Yeah. Something to think about, but we have time."

She wound her arms around me and leaned in. What started as a sweet kiss, quickly escalated as things often did with us. Before I knew it, we were undressed, and I was inside her as she straddled me on the futon.

Little did we know, we would find out about babies between us sooner than we thought.

ROYAL BASTARDS CODE

PROTECT: The club and your brothers come before anything else and must be protected at all costs. CLUB is FAMILY.

RESPECT: Earn it & Give it. Respect club law. Respect the patch. Respect your brothers. Disrespect a member and there will be hell to pay.

HONOR: Being patched in is an honor, not a right. Your colors are sacred, not to be left alone, and NEVER let them touch the ground.

OL' LADIES: Never disrespect a member's or brother's ol' lady. PERIOD.

CHURCH is MANDATORY.

LOYALTY: Takes precedence over all, including well-being.

HONESTY: Never LIE, CHEAT, or STEAL from another member or the club.

TERRITORY: You are to respect your brothers' property and follow their Chapter's club rules.

TRUST: Years to earn it… seconds to lose it.

NEVER RIDE OFF: Brothers do not abandon their family.

ACKNOWLEDGEMENTS

This time, I'm starting fresh. I tend to be incredibly redundant in this section and I apologize, but there are certain people who are there with me through the various steps of the writing process. I hate leaving them out, but by now, I think most of them know who they are.

With that being said, I first want to thank you the reader. Without you, there would be little point in publishing. Sure, I could write all day, every day, but if no one wanted to read it... well, you get the picture. Each time one of you reaches out and thanks me for my words or tells me how much you loved a certain book, I am humbled and blow away. Because I never thought I'd be "that author." You know, the one people actually read.

Next, I want to thank my daughter, **Rhiannon**. Though she doesn't read my books, she's been an awesome support system. Crazy to think that my little girl is all grown up and can handle talk about "grown up things." LOL. She has helped me flesh out and plot a story that I'm trying to organize on more than one occasion. She lets me bounce ideas of her and tells me when I've chosen a name that "sucks." But most of all, she's been proud of me when I don't feel I've done a damn thing to be proud of. So thanks for growing up to be a really amazing adult human, Rhiannon.

Thank you to those of you who have reached out to me on my social media platforms, via my website, or by email. To think that you took a portion of your day to write to me is heartwarming. Even those of you who were mad at me for the way a story went or because I changed how my books were offered. LOL.

Thank you to those of you who have recommended my books on BookBub, Goodreads, and through social media groups. Reviews and recommendations are the LIFEBLOOD of and indie author. I cannot stress enough how awesome it is that you took the time to do that for me or any other author.

Pam, **Kristin**, **Brenda**, and **Lisa**, you guys are the best. From beta reading, to promoting, to cheerleading, y'all are my girls. Thank you and everyone else who shares my posts—whether they were preorders, new releases, or simply something of mine you thought was pretty cool.

Glenna, your patience with my "can we move this a little" or my "what if we did this" requests is beyond measure. Thank you for taking my visions and breathing life into them to make beautiful covers. You're the bombdiggity and I love you bunches!

Wander, you and my checking account have a seriously toxic relationship, but your talent behind the lens is immeasurable! LOL. Thank you for another incredible image!

Thane, this image… *chef's kiss* You are the perfect Ares and I thank you from the bottom of my heart for allowing it to grace my cover.

Then, a huge *thank you* goes out to my family who brag about me being an author (despite the genre in which I write!) and for always believing in me. In the beginning, I wasn't sure if I would tell any of you that I was writing, but your amazing support has touched me. Though, I often wonder if you know exactly what I write or if your friends read my books and are traumatized. Bahahaha!

If this is my first book you've read, you may not know who he is, but a huge thank you goes out to **PSH**, my very own "Porn Star Hubby" (if you ever meet me, or friend me on social media, ask me to tell you the story). He's the best book schlepper, one man cheerleading squad, and pimp-er of my books that ever walked the earth. Love you bunches, babe.

Penny. Once upon a time there was a girl who didn't believe in herself. Then came a red-headed girl that smacked the first girl upside the head and said, "You can do this!" Thank you for believing in me enough for both of us in the beginning and always. You are never surprised at my success and that is humbling. Congratulations on surviving nursing school! Now believe me when I tell you that you are going to be a rock star of a nurse. Love you, boo!

Stacey of Champagne Book Design, you are and forever will be a goddess! I know I'm a pain, but you've stuck with me through thick and thin. Thank you for making my pages a work of art and for being so understanding of my "don't kill me" messages and emails. LMAO.

The ladies of Kristine's Krazy Fangirls, y'all are the best. You're the lovers of my books, the ones that I share my funny stories with, the ones who cheer me on when I'm struggling with a book I promised you, and I love you all to pieces! (((BIG HUGS)))! I can't thank you enough for your comments, your support, and your love of all things books. Come join us if you're not part of the group www.facebook.com/groups/kristineskrazyfangirls

Often, I try to spin the military into my books. This is for many reasons. Because of those reasons, my last, but never least, is a massive thank you to America's servicemen and women who protect our freedom on a daily basis. They do their duty, leaving their families for weeks, months, and years at a time, without asking for praise or thanks. I would also like to remind the readers that not all combat injuries are visible, nor do they heal easily. These silent, wicked injuries wreak havoc on their minds and hearts while we go about our days completely oblivious. Thank you all for your service.

OTHER BOOKS BY
KRISTINE ALLEN

Demented Sons MC Series - Iowa

Colton's Salvation

Mason's Resolution

Erik's Absolution

Kayde's Temptation

Snow's Addiction

Straight Wicked Series

Make Music With Me

Snare My Heart

No Treble Allowed

String Me Up

Demented Sons MC Series - Texas

Lock and Load

Styx and Stones

Smoke and Mirrors

Jax and Jokers

Got Your Six (Formerly in Remember Ryan Anthology)

RBMC - Ankeny Iowa

Voodoo

Angel

A Very Venom Christmas

Chains

Haunting Ghost

Charming Phoenix

Sabre

Facet (Coming Soon!)

RBMC - Dallas Texas

Taming Raptor

Raptor's Revenge

Sparking Ares

The Iced Series

Hooking

Tripping

Roughing

Holding

Fighting Love

Heels, Rhymes, & Nursery Crimes

Roses Are Red (RBMC connection)

Violets Are Blue (Coming Soon!)

Pinched and Cuffed Duet with M. Merin

The Weight of Honor

The Weight of Blood (by M. Merin)

ABOUT THE AUTHOR

Kristine Allen lives in beautiful Central Texas with her adoring husband. They have four brilliant, wacky, and wonderful children. She is surrounded by twenty-six acres, where her five horses, four dogs, and five cats run the place. She's a hockey addict and feeds that addiction with season tickets to the Texas Stars. Kristine realized her dream of becoming a contemporary romance author after years of reading books like they were going out of style and having her own stories running rampant through her head. She works as a night shift nurse, but in stolen moments, taps out ideas and storylines until they culminate in characters and plots that pull her readers in and keep them entranced for hours.

Reviews are the life blood of an indie author. If you enjoyed this story, please consider leaving a review on the sales channel of your choice, bookbub.com, goodreads.com, allauthor.com, or your favorite review platform, to share your experience with other interested readers. Thank you! <3

Follow Kristine on:

Facebook www.facebook.com/kristineallenauthor

Instagram www.instagram.com/_kristine_allen_

Twitter @KAllenAuthor

TikTok: www.tiktok.com/@kristineallenauthor

All Author www.kristineallen.allauthor.com

BookBub www.bookbub.com/authors/kristine-allen

Goodreads www.goodreads.com/kristineallenauthor

Webpage www.kristineallenauthor.com

Made in United States
North Haven, CT
04 January 2023

30577819R00107